# TIME PIMP

# GARRETT COOK

Eraserhead Press
Portland, OR

ERASERHEAD PRESS
205 NE BRYANT
PORTLAND, OR 97211

WWW.ERASERHEADPRESS.COM

ISBN: 1-62105-118-8

Printed in the USA.

*To Miss Ginger,*
*Allons Y!*

TIME

PIMP

# OPERATION

# FLORENCE

*The Planet Netzach*

The Purple Cadillac came to a stop and the Italian poet Dante Alighieri stepped out of it, onto streets that were constantly sighing. He looked up into rose pink skies to see the world lit not by a Sun but by a reclining nude giantess in the sky. The driver of the car, a tall man, well dressed and bronze as gods stepped out afterwards. He was attired in a purple velvet suit uncreasable, devoid of stains or wrinkles or signs of imperfection. His hat was black, crushed velvet apparently, with a feather in it that constantly shifted colors like a fickle chameleon. His eyes were hidden by shades with lenses so black it seemed incomprehensible that there'd be anything but lenses behind them. In one hand, he held a stylish golden cane, the head of which was carved into the face of a rabbit. The other, he placed on Dante's shoulder.

"Mister Dahn-tay, welcome, to Netzach."

The poet fell to his knees weeping and the rose pink streets manifested minute mouths to drink his tears. They let out moans of delight.

"Signor Time Pimp, this place, it is too beautiful, too delightful for a wretch like me who would need the help…of a panderer."

The driver, Time Pimp, was taken aback.

"Panderer! You'd best check yourself before you wreck yourself, Guido!"

Dante rose to his feet.

"My humblest apologies, Signor Time Pimp, I did not mean…"

Time Pimp crossed his arms.

"You are lucky, Client, that you ain't one of my hos."

The Italian nodded solemnly and returned to taking in the scenery. Insects of luminescence were flying around him, copulating, making shapes, runes and letters with their bodies of pure light. On the sidewalks of Netzach, saxophones walked on shapely androgynous night black-legs pumping smoky suggestions into the already moist and welcoming atmosphere. The smell of sweat and Agua Florida hung thick in the air.

Time Pimp allowed a smile to cross his delicate yet masculine face.

"And as for you seeking out a pimp, it was me who sought you out, Client. I go where my shoes tell me."

With the cane, he pointed down to his platform shoes. A small octopus was swimming in a pale green liquid in each shoe. Their tiny black eyes were full of wisdom and contentment. The poet had to wonder what it would be like to live in a man's shoes and to sleep and dream there.

"I do not understand, Signor Time Pimp, what made the Lord send you, but I am happy that you have brought me to this place in Heaven."

Time Pimp laughed and shook his head.

"Don't know how a jiveass motherfucker like yourself changed the Western Canon of Earth Literature singlehandedly."

Dante looked at Time Pimp befuddled.

"You'll see. We just gotta find you some action so you can get out of this slump and write your masterpiece. Shouldn't be long. I got a house right around the corner."

Dante and Time Pimp walked down the streets of Netzach, taking in the scents, listening to the saxophone music and occasionally staring up in admiration at the voluptuous slumbering sun. They passed by a series of houses and shops whose walls were live flowers, whispering flowers, pheromone flowers of sweetness and nostalgia. Reluctant smiles came and went from Time Pimp's face and tears struggled out of the already overworked eyes of the great Italian poet.

Finally they turned a corner and Time Pimp stopped in front of a thick wall of whispering roses.

"It's me," he said to the wall. And the roses parted, revealing a golden door with a rabbit head and a dollar sign engraved on it. He tapped the door with his cane and it opened, leading into an antechamber full of hookahs and bean bag chairs. The room was surrounded by doors, each depicting a man, woman or what to Dante could only be a devil of some kind. There were women with heads like ants, women in fancy white dresses with powdered wigs, women in bejeweled lingerie, women in plate mail, women riding naked on tigers, lascivious nuns, big strapping naked lads with paddles or whips in their hands, mechanical girls, ladies conjoined at their exquisite heads with other ladies, ape-like men hunched over and clad in animal skins. Dante wondered what all of these doors could mean and what they led to. Could it be possible that this mysterious panderer actually had such bizarre wares to sample?

A tall woman, her body crafted apparently from red bricks, which contrasted greatly with the black nightgown that clung so tightly to it, entered the room through a door that bore her likeness. She handed Time Pimp a wad of money. He nodded.

"It's all here. You done good, Julissa."

He smacked her soundly on the ass. Dante felt he must have been exceptional at slapping, for the slap actually made a sound in spite of her brick skin. She smiled, then, seeing Dante, her mouth opened wide.

"Is that…"

"Bitch, you know I got the best client list in history. Fact, history is my black book and you know it."

"Sho nuff, Time Pimp."

Time Pimp gestured at her with his cane.

"You interested, Guido? She's a bit jagged, might cut yourself on them titties but I ain't had a customer complain yet."

Dante rose, clasping Julissa's brick hand.

"Signorina, you are most certainly quite lovely. But I do not know if you, or any woman, is for me this day. My heart is full of sadness and I long for one who is lost."

A perplexed Julissa turned to Time Pimp.

"You sure you've got the right Client, Playa? This guy seems like a lost cause."

Time Pimp pointed his cane at Julissa. The cane emitted a humming noise and Julissa's brick body trembled with ecstasy. She let out a series of loud moans of satisfaction. She took her brick breasts in her hand massaging them, revealing to an astonished Dante that they were surprisingly pliant. A drop of wet cement from between her legs fell to the whorehouse floor.

"Bitch, I am Time Pimp and you best recognize that I and my shoes do not lie and I do not make mistakes. Dante Alighieri is gonna get hisself laid and I am gonna get myself paid, ho."

The poet placed his hand over his mouth in shock and terror. He had seen a great many things he had not understood, but this display was possibly the most chilling. The cane's sorcery seemed to have the power to stir a woman's body to sin. Walking about Netzach, he had thought himself in Heaven, but now had little reason to believe he was not in the presence of the Devil himself.

"Please, signor Time Pimp, do not do her any more harm on my account! Have mercy, Signor Time Pimp!"

Julissa rose from the floor, threw her head back and laughed heartily. Time Pimp joined her.

"Bitch Julissa, fetch Client and I a gingerbread house."

"Get yo own damn gingerbread house, playa!"

Time Pimp pulled back his cane threateningly. He would not be deprived of a delicious gingerbread house. Though made of bricks, Julissa ran like the wind through a door marked with a gingerbread house. Time Pimp let out a confident boisterous laugh.

"Ah, the orgone cane makes the bitches come running, can me 'em cum and it can make 'em run!"

"I do not know what to make of this Signor Time Pimp," said the concerned poet, "I am not certain I can keep the company of witches in good conscience. I am a magistrate and a man of faith, it's bad enough that you are a…a…" Dante struggled with the word.

Time Pimp heaved a sigh.

"Mister Dahn-tay, there is no shame in being a pimp and I most assuredly ain't no witch. We are in space and in the future. I am no witch and Julissa is no demon. She has it hard. She comes from a place where there are so few resources that people have changed themselves. Their whole lives revolve around building things. And they build these things out of each other. She lived a hard life before I offered her this way out."

Dante tried to wrap his head around the idea of being in

the future. He could not imagine tomorrow being a place or yesterday or last Tuesday or the Birth of Christ. He realized fully at that moment that he had been brought where he had been brought in a magical flying machine, that he was suspended somewhere beyond the sky and that there was a place where people, if they could even be called that, built buildings from each other. He grew dizzy and had to struggle not to faint. If his host was speaking the truth he was a generous and formidable man.

"I have never heard anything so strange, so sad. I cannot conceive of such an awful place. It would surely be a hell on Earth. And this lady, she is brave as she is lovely if she survived and thrived there. You have done her a great service, Signor Time Pimp."

Julissa returned from the gingerbread house door carrying a gingerbread mansion and two shotglasses full of water. She set it down on the floor and handed Dante and Time Pimp a glass apiece. She did not stick around but rather dashed for the door marked with the brick woman.

Time Pimp greedily tore off a piece of the mansion's wall and took a pronounced bite.

"What a future," he said, "where two men can eat a whole house."

Dante laughed uncomfortably and broke off a wall of his own, crunching down on it. He was surprised by how much he liked the food in this strange place. Time Pimp grabbed Dante's shotglass from him. He held it in front of his face. Time Pimp's facial muscles seemed to tremble, his body shook a bit, not like the shaking of the brick prostitute but still a heavy shake. He let out a deep breath and suddenly, where once there was water, there was a fine brandy, which he handed back to the Italian.

The Italian's mouth gaped open.

"Signor Time Pimp, you are as Jesus Christ!"

Time Pimp laughed.

"It's only alchemy, Client. I just psychically cause the atoms to emit a pheromone that attracts different atoms, which make sweet love-making the water turn into delicious cognac."

"Then sir, you could turn lead into gold!"

Time Pimp shook his head.

"No sir, Mister Dahn-tay, a pimp can only make money pimpin'. Else I attract the wrath of the galactic pimp council."

"Oh," said Dante, grabbing more gingerbread house instead of trying to find out what any of that meant.

Time Pimp tapped his cane on the floor and several doors opened, and from them there came a series of young women of many races wearing clothing from many times and places, all of whom prostrated themselves before Time Pimp. A cowgirl tipped her hat, harem girls planted kisses upon his platform shoes, medieval courtesans curtsied, a flapper went down on one knee, a heavy browed cavegirl in a sabertooth bikini pounded her ample chest in a primitive salute, a geisha bowed deeply. The numbers of chambers that still remained unopened were a testament to the sheer size of Time Pimp's momentous stable of hos.

"Ladies, it is always a pleasure," said Time Pimp, tipping his hat to reveal a giant purple pompadour underneath it. It was a hairstyle that inspired trembling, a hairstyle fit for such a powerful leader of men and seller of women as Time Pimp. One at a time, the girls reached out tremulously, placing a hand on the hairdo as if it were a holy relic that would cure all of their ailments. They closed their eyes solemnly, reflecting upon the hairdo's meaning. Some of the girls sobbed quietly. Dante sobbed quietly as well. Who was this man whose hair had such divine majesty as all of this?

"Client," said Time Pimp, "take your pick."

One at a time, the ladies from all over time stood before Dante, planting kisses on his cheek, then falling to their knees before him. The poet got the blessing of Viking spearmaidens, geishas, harem girls, cowgirls, a cave girl, a flapper, courtesans and serving wenches. He had never imagined such a bounty of affection and such a world of possibilities. He turned away, crying.

"Signor Time Pimp," said Dante, "dismiss these women. I am just a humble poet, an undeserving wretch and the desire they fill me with betrays my lost love!"

Time Pimp thunderously struck the floor with his cane three times. The very house seemed to shake with his pimpish wrath. The women scattered, returning to the doors they emerged from and thus the chambers behind them. Not a one wanted to stick around and tempt fate by protesting to the client or Time Pimp.

"Ingrate." Time Pimp gritted his gold teeth. He reached into the gingerbread house pulling out a gingerbread pimp and biting its delicious head off. Just as he liked eating houses, he was always cheered up by eating himself in effigy, but not this time. Time Pimp was upset and thoroughly disappointed.

"What have I done to deserve this?"

Dante turned around, placing a consoling hand upon the pimp's shoulder.

"Signor Time Pimp, you had the noblest of intentions, though whoremongering is a cardinal sin. You only wished to free me from the grief of losing my beloved Beatrice. But you cannot. She is dead and I will never see her again and I cannot bear to think of touching another woman. I thank you, Signor for your affections and your noblest effort."

"I don't need your pity, sucka. I ain't paid and you ain't laid!"

"There is no splendor on Earth or in Heaven so precious as my lost Beatrice, Signor Time Pimp."

Time Pimp lifted his cane over his head, body twitching with anger. He cared very little that he was about to bring it down upon one of history's finest poets, the author of the Interno. He would, with the orgone cane, show that the pimp was the true master of Heaven and Hell. He had come through history to offer this man consolation and solace to make his work and to show that the pimp race was a generous and glorious one. And he had turned down his hos and he had turned down his future and his displays of power. It was not often Time Pimp would strike down a client, but he felt ready at this moment.

It was a signal from his shoes that spared the Italian master the thrashing of a lifetime at the hands of the angry pimp. The psychic octopi were very insistent that Time Pimp move on and not hesitate a moment before returning to 13<sup>th</sup> Century Florence. Already enraged at Dante, Time Pimp was now angry at his shoes as well. He could not understand what they found so goddamn urgent that he couldn't punish a fool for wasting his time.

"Come on, Guido," he said, voice weighed down by disappointment, I'm gonna take you home."

"Mille grazie, Signor Time Pimp."

"Whatever."

So, they returned together to the streets of Netzach and the purple Cadillac. Time Pimp placed the key in the ignition and set the controls for Florence of the 13<sup>th</sup> Century. And at that, the pink tunnel appeared from thin air. Giant concentric circles of light, it opened, inviting the Cadillac inside. The walls of the tunnel were fleshy and inside it, hot funky music blared. The noise was a bit disturbing to the Italian and yet he felt an inexplicable desire to wave his hands in the air with wild, unexpected abandon. The air was moist, pungent, oddly meaty and the poet found beads of dew condensing on his face. He lapped drops from the side of his mouth and felt relaxed. His eyes rolled back in his head and his genitals stirred as much as they had in the presence of Time Pimp's stable of hos.

When they emerged from the tunnel, life was different.

Florence, 1288

"Destination reached, Playa," said the car's mechanical voice, but it did not seem to be so. Thirteenth century Florence was not a place where lionheaded children rode naked men down dirty streets whose gutters overflowed with blood. Nor was it a place where lionfaces on hundred foot television screens mounted above spikes of impaled bodies announced "GIVE MORE!" It was not a place where lionheaded reptiles, whose scaly forms were covered in undulating quills, plucked human organs from bony trees, eagerly devouring them. Though Florence had been a city in torment and one where in the poet's eyes sin had run rampant, it had not been a place of such grotesquerie as all of this.

Time Pimp's jaw dropped. His shoes let out an audible whimper. Dante struggled with the sights and the smells, struggled to stay conscious, struggled to stay sane. He wondered how he could when the indomitable unflappable Time Pimp was prepared to give in to despair completely.

"No," Time Pimp begged nobody in particular, "not these guys. Not the Lionheads! NOT THE LIONHEADS!"

He let out a scream and the cane too let out a shriek. He had almost let anger over take him back in the Netzach whorehouse and terror was starting to get to him now. It was not becoming behavior for a pimp. It was the opposite of cool but he couldn't help it. There were organ trees growing in the city streets of one of his favorite cities on one of his favorite planets. He'd eaten minestrone with da Vinci, had a threesome together with a whore whose enigmatic smile inspired the Mona Lisa, a woman he had to add to his stable and one of his favorites. He knew this place to be a height of art and culture, and a pimp was to at all times be refined and knowledgeable. Two lionhead children on naked male steeds whispered between themselves, pointing at Time Pimp and Dante, who realized in unison that there was only time for running and not nostalgia.

"I thought you said that you would bring me home," said Dante as they tried to dash from sight.

"This is the Earth," Time Pimp replied grimly, "this is your city."

"I do not understand. How did they come here, why?"

They ran together past a series of glass buildings where crying old men teetering on metal chicken legs simply could not stop themselves from performing gruesome surgeries, extracting body parts from screaming men and women. One could not incidentally look into a window of this new Florence without seeing this occurring. Most of the city seemed to have been repurposed for this intent. At least it would seem so, until sneaking through an alley that had been familiar to the both of them, they saw the pens. Grisly though the sight was, Dante and Time Pimp had to stop and watch to see what was going on.

In the pens, armless men were joylessly fucking armless women whose tear-stained faces pleaded for mercy, pleaded for the men to stop. Blood was running down their legs from constant misuse of their sexes. The men almost certainly wished to stop, but did not have these options. Lionheads were behind them, watching them, when they tried to stop or when their beleaguered cocks softened and slipped out, the squirming quills of the lionheads, poked into them and the lionheads glowed with bioelectricity, sending volts into the reluctant studs through their organic tasers. If one collapsed, a juvenile lionhead would grab them, dragging them through the street on their slavesteed, no doubt to be taken to be harvested by the old men in the panoptic hospitals.

Dante grabbed hold of Time Pimp's suit.

"Signore, this cannot be! Tell me what these devils are and how they came here!"

Time Pimp removed Dante's hands from his suit. Even under this duress, nobody was to touch the velvet.

"They're called the lionheads. Long ago, they enslaved and killed everything on their home planet, drained it of resources. They built too fast, killed too many too soon. Ecosystems just can't take 'em. So they have no home. They just wander through timestreams, showing up, using everything good, building shitty cities and moving on. They've been here about three years. This place has maybe one more before it's a smoking heap of shit and organs. I hate 'em cause they get in on my game. Everybody gets down for free and nobody enjoys themselves. Pimp's worst nightmare. Nobody wins. No respect for the game."

"So what do we do?"

Time Pimp shrugged.

"I'm a pimp. My job is to get paid and get folks laid and make history happy. I think we should get back to the car and see if we can find an Earth whose time stream hasn't been fucked up by these lames."

Dante gave Time Pimp the judgmental gaze, the hellward gaze seen in all the sculptures and paintings of him. This was not the sad, grieving man he had met but the ferocious one who had called him time and city to task and sentenced hypocrites to worse than burning.

"I had thought you were a good man, but you are nothing but a pimp. You are a panderer and a coward."

Dante took the purse from his belt, tossing it at Time Pimp.

"You get paid for your efforts, taking me away from my world so I did not have to see it becoming this."

"You ungrateful, you can stay…"

Time Pimp stopped midsentence, noticing that there were three mounted lionhead children only a few feet behind him dragging unconscious slaves. All feline eyes were upon him.

"You do not look like you are of this time," said a lionhead child in a high, effeminate voice. "The Impatience does not permit time travelers in his streams."

"Yes," said a second one, shrill but deadpan, "time travelers are poop."

"I want his hat," said the third in a rumbling baritone.

"Back off, lames!" Time Pimp raised his orgone cane, "I'm gonna set the cane to pain!"

The lionhead children did not back off. The cane shook, emitting an angry hiss. Dante felt a wave of heat and discomfort coming from the strange device and felt deeply glad he had not managed to offend Time Pimp to the point where force was involved. The cane was a devastating force for pain or for pleasure and to get in the way of its wielder could only be called sheer folly.

But nonetheless, the young lionheads seemed undeterred.

"What is pain? We do not understand this. Surrender your weapon and your time travel vessel. The Impatience does not want any slaves escaping."

"Ain't nobody gonna take no slaves from here," Time Pimp hissed through gold-capped teeth, "I'm gonna get into my Cadillac and I'm gonna leave this jiveass time behind, and you should count yoself lucky, lame, that you don't get cut none for messin' with my game!"

Four adult lionheads joined the children.

"What have you found, Winston?" asked one whose multiple scaly teats indicated that she was a female.

"I have found a time traveler, homecunt," said the one with the deep voice.

19

"It was I who found him," said the first lionhead to speak, "Winston is a puppycoddling liar. He wants extra fistings again. It's I who get the fistings!"

"Homecunt fist no tattletale," said the second, still unaffected, "not for time travelers. Time travelers are poop."

"I am homecunt of this squadron," said the scaleteated grown up, "I fist who I choose. Any more protestations and arguing you go sleephole with no kidneys, puppycoddling apefaced small things. On homeworld we had no steeds fine as these! You get fine slaves and you go apefaced! Death's too good."

Another adult lionhead cleared its throat.

"We cannot mew about who is homecunt and who is not! We have a time traveler in our midst and time travelers mean trouble. The Impatience would not want this to be. We must kill this time traveler or bring this time traveler to The Impatience for killing!"

"I want to kill the time traveler!" cried the baritone lionhead child.

"NO! I will kill the time traveler!" the first lionhead child protested, "I found him so he will die by my hand and homecunt shall fist me mightily for all I've done!"

"You get no fisting at all!" screamed the female, "None will reward you for being a nuisance! It is the business of grown things to bring time travelers to The Impatience or kill them."

"You know," said a greenfurred lionhead, "we don't get time travelers very often at all."

"You sound stupid!" said the female lionhead, "Whatever you would say is boring!"

The male lionhead in the front of the group who spoke first slashed the female in the face with his claws making her gush magenta blood. He lapped this off her wound. The female went down on all fours. The male looked past her to address the other two; the green furred one and a particularly large, smelly, specimen.

"We do get few time travelers. If we deprive The Impatient..." The male lionhead was cut off.

Time Pimp had pointed the cane at the male lionhead's back and let loose another burst of pain. Perhaps the children simply lacked the complex nervous system to experience the orgone cane's activation of their pain receptors. At least, as he sent out waves of pain from the rabbit head, he hoped this was so. The lionhead twitched for a moment. He scrunched his nose and sniffed the air.

"What was that?" one of the quills on his side shifted, pointing directly at Time Pimp.

"I think it's a weapon," said the greenfurred lionhead.

"You are wise in your years, elder. I hope you hurry up and die."

Time Pimp bent back, readying both the cane for if they came closer and his right hand to slap any comers.

"Listen here, bitches, ain't none of you going to kill my ass or take me to your leader. I'm ready to fight all seven of you."

An impetuous child spurred his slave on, "riding" at Time Pimp, who axekicked the child's slavesteed in the head, his platform shoe landing with a loud crunch, bringing the slave to the ground and the lionhead child as well. Time Pimp did not hesitate to push one of the shoe's five inch heels into the prostrate juvenile lionhead's throat, pull his foot away and then stomp down again. Hard. And again and again and again. The little lionhead gasped, then breathed its last.

"Time travelers are poop!" screamed the second one, preparing to come at Time Pimp, but the female lionhead rose to her feet, grabbing the child by the scruff of his neck and stopping him from attacking.

"This is not for children! The time traveler can fight!"

The third one backed away, letting the adults advance on Time Pimp and Dante. Dante's eyes were closed and his hands folded in prayer. The male and the gigantic lionhead led the charge, with the greenfurred one bringing up the rear. With a mighty backhand, Time Pimp sent the male lionhead flying backward. The pimp hand technique had extracted funds from history's toughest johns and hos, and Time Pimp had refined it well. Even though the orgone cane could not show them what pain was, Time Pimp's martial arts skills certainly could.

But the big one closed quickly, quills thrusting out at the angry pimp and arms extended to wrap around him. Time Pimp stomped hard on the big lionhead's foot with his fatal platform but even though he heard the snapping of bones, the lionhead 1stood its ground and in standing its ground, was able to poke Time Pimp with one of its quills, through it releasing a great deal of electrical current. Time Pimp's body shuddered but still he had enough muscle control to smack the lionhead in the side of its face with the cane. It was a mighty smack and a smaller more timid beast or something aware of the concept of pain might have given way. But this was a lionhead and an exceptionally large one. Even as the platforms came down hard on both his feet, he did nothing to show that he suffered at all.

The green lionhead had closed in on Dante, stabbing him with one of its quills and biotasering him. The poet's eyes remained closed and hands folded, even as electricity coursed through him, knocking him out. He did not have Time Pimp's pimpish physiology to protect him, he was but a flesh and blood man afflicted by alien electricity. The greenfurred lionhead draped the poet over his shoulder as Time Pimp struggled to survive the bearhug and bioelectric shock pulsing through him.

Time Pimp's powerful pimpcane pounding grew weaker, his struggle against the electrified lionheaded space reptile more feeble. The stomping got cut off, the idle attempts to cave in knees with powerful kicks came to a halt. The pimp's thunderous ferocity died down to whispers until at last, his energy waned, his flesh sizzled, his eyes grew dark and his mind went blank. Time Pimp collapsed and was triumphantly carried off by his big, smelly, powerful assailant.

Time Pimp was sitting in a naked man's lap. Though the man's feet had been nailed to the floor and his arms had spikes through them, the lolling and rolling of the tongueless, eyeless man's head indicated that somehow he had still been kept alive. Time Pimp's arms had been bound to the man's by a thread of loose intestine running up through the floor.

Dante was beside him, bound in the same manner to a woman existing in the same state. If the city that had gone up over Florence had not been proof enough of the depravity of the lionheads, their ugliness and their cruelty, than this method of bondage would have sufficed. And were that not enough, then the sight of their leader, The Impatience, would certainly do the trick.

The Impatience, twice the size of a regular lionhead, sat upon a giant, throne of discarded meat and organs. Two squirming infants were sewn to its oversized feet, serving as shoes. The quills of his freakishly large body reached out to spear hearts and livers and kidneys, bringing them up to its mouths. The Impatience had three of these mouths, three faces conjoined, one pointing to the left, one to the right and one straight ahead, each slavering for meat and each sated by a quill bringing speared meat to its leonine jaws. Each head finished ripping and chewing and tearing a vanquished and lost human heart before the front head addressed its grimly bound captives.

"I see you are awake, time traveler. This pleases me. I do not like to wait to make my needs and sentiments known. For as you may know, I am The Impatience. I am easily bored, angered and displeased. These are the traits that allowed me to evolve into this position and into the perfect being before you."

"You lionheads got some fool ideas about perfection," spat Time Pimp, "Fool!"

The three heads laughed.

"Nothing is wrong if I benefit," said the one on the left, "and anyone who thinks otherwise is truly a fool. Such thoughts invite failure and annihilation, which is beneficial to me so in that way, they are not wrong. I will grow fatter and crueler from their fruits. This is how ignorance feeds me. All are either wise enough to recognize my virtue and that of my philosophy or they are foolish enough to underestimate me and so shall feed me. This is what makes us unstoppable."

Time Pimp laughed back.

"That's what makes you a chump! Everything you ever

have, you waste it you wreck it or you eat it! You're a sucker and you're weak. Everything you got's gonna be gone because you can't wait to play with it!"

The right head growled. The left head laughed. The one facing straight ahead argued.

"Nothing is wasted if I use it. Nothing is played with and broken soon enough. I can see from your clothes that you are a pimp. Highly amusing that you would speak ill of The Impatience's philosophy."

Time Pimp's orgone cane was right at his feet. Though thus far no lionheads had proven vulnerable to it, he felt he had to give it a try again. He struggled against his bonds and tried to be subtle in his grasping for the dangerous weapon nearby. He realized immediately that he would have to keep The Impatience stalled long enough to get the weapon into his hand and find a setting that could do something about the lionhead menace.

"Why is it amusing that I wouldn't believe the universe exists so you can conquer it and waste it? Do you think pimps waste life?"

"You are an exploiter and a wrecker of lives, Time Pimp. All things are customers or resources you can use to make yourself richer. You use up your whores until they can be used no longer. The pimp and the lionhead are not so different…"

The head on the left smiled.

"…Time Pimp."

Time Pimp kept trying to reach his orgone cane. He wished he could do something about the bonds on him, that pimpish alchemy could work on organic matter. He did not like The Impatience's implications and he certainly didn't like that the lionheads knew who he was.

"My business is never done dirty. The ho is happy, the client is happy and I am happy. Everyone is happy! Pimpin' makes the worlds go 'round, baby! I ain't nothin' like your people-eatin' ass! "

The Impatience put his front snout in the air.

"You use human capital. I use human capital. Both of us have fabulous shoes. You build your fortune on sex and power,

I build my fortune on sex and power. We are the same. There is no debate and I tire of having one. I am The Impatience and I am going to make you an offer. You will not refuse it. You are selfish and violent, a credit to your race's values. I wish to harness this. I have an offer."

Dante's eyes opened and the poet let out a cutting primal scream. He closed his eyes and whispered prayers, searched his memory for the face of the one whose loss had made this grief that Time Pimp so unsuccessfully sought to assuage. This creature before could only be one being, a creature he hoped his prayers would liberate him from. Dante opened his eyes again, only to look pleadingly at Time Pimp.

"Signor Time Pimp, you must stand strong against this fiend. You must never let him break your soul."

Time Pimp listened to Dante, but knew also that he still had to play for time and to come up with a way out.

"What kind of offer? If I'm going to deal with an ugly sonofabitch like you, I gots to get paid, Mister Three Different Lions!"

Dante was mortified.

"You can't! You cannot possibly…"

"Client, be silent!" Time Pimp reprimanded the Italian, "let the man speak his minds."

"Yes, apeface, the affairs we speak of are above the mewling cowardly, redblooded concerns of your race. These are the province of gods. I want you to take your time travel device and we will plant a beacon in it. You will go through the time streams, letting us know which worlds are most ripe for exploitation and ruin for feeding the lionhead empire. It is not so much an offer as the alternative is quite grisly."

"If you know 'bout pimps you know we don't tolerate threats."

"I am The Impatience. I do not traffic in threats. They waste my time. As I know you are Time Pimp, I am aware of your counterpart and the position that he holds and his agendas. Knowing his agendas, I know well that he is very much in need of something we have been working on. I think you know what I am referring to. Indeed, the Pantemporal

Annihilator is admittedly not within our grasp, but we have a prototype for something that will certainly do for us in a pinch."

Time Pimp's jaw dropped.

"You wouldn't! You can't!"

The three heads laughed and yowled.

"I can. I will. If you decline. Your choices are the following: becoming my agent and find me juicy streams and planets to overbuild and pick clean or I can activate the Perpetual Torment and Suffering Device that you and the human poet are strapped to. And I can send your counterpart the schematics. I'm sure he'd be very interested in them and they'll no doubt help his research division build the machine he actually needs. You have very little time to decide. I am not called The Impatience for nothing."

Dante spoke softly, his voice tender and compassionate.

"You cannot take this monster's offer. There is far too much at stake."

Time Pimp sighed.

"You don't understand, Client, this is Perpetual Torment. And I know that I've taken his offer because we're not experiencing that right now. I can't accept perpetual torment."

Dante nodded in acknowledgement, but stood firm.

"If we don't, then the entire world must. And more worlds still. You say you bring pleasure? You say you make people happy? Then this is the time to prove it. We have no choice. You must refuse, in his offer there is also perpetual torment."

"I hate you," said Time Pimp.

"And for good reason," said the poet solemnly.

"You are making a grave mistake," growled The Impatience's right face.

"What you would do cannot be undone," said the left.

"Are you really such a fool as all this?" asked the front face.

"Juice us up, you ugly three-faced sucka!" Time Pimp said and prepared himself for Perpetual Torment as best he could, which was very little as he was about to face Perpetual Torment. And the lionheads juiced them up.

Time Pimp expected a pain that would wrack him, as it was a pain that would extend through his whole history. He expected to feel his body betraying him or his guts opening up or his testicles caved in by a perpetual boot. Though he had lived a great long time, he had not sufficiently contemplated Perpetual Torment. He had not thought he would come face to face with it, since it being Perpetual Torment projected through his time stream, he could only know it forever or know it never. Time Pimp did not know or care how time travel worked. More or less nobody did regardless of how often they did it. Time travel is very complicated.

Perpetual Torment brought him to a place he had conceived of but never known. Perhaps he would go there someday. Perhaps the going itself was the nature of Perpetual Torment. The Netzach sun was dead in the sky, splayed open and whatever made her luminous had been taken out. The music on the streets was silent, the smell of coconut cigarillos, anal lube and promise replaced by something that was almost spraypaint but not quite. The buildings, once all sentient flowers, were quarantine tents. Perfect Netzach, Netzach of music, Netzach of lust was quiet and lustless and devoid of the pungent and womanly smells.

He continued down the streets a man possessed, a man with no control over his stride and no means of escape. He should have had no desire to see this place become what it had become and to know the full ramifications of a planet with a dead sun and no song and no lust. He should have felt like getting back in the purple Cadillac and fleeing until this nightmare was out of sight forever. But this was Perpetual Torment, coursing through every moment of his being. So he kept exploring, though the Netzach he loved would never be his again.

A few blocks into his journey, Time Pimp found himself no longer alone. The streets were not empty but filled with beings. He knew that they were human, but one not familiar with their manner of dress would have thought otherwise. They would have thought that under the head-to-toe latex that concealed their features, the shapes of their bodies, all the finer points of their anatomy, there could not possibly be human beings. Human beings would not relinquish their faces, hide their expressions, hide their curves, hide their selfhood, shield themselves completely from touch. Human beings were visceral creatures and an individualistic race that took great pride in their beauty, their selfhood and their distinctiveness. This was why, in spite of all the exotic, erotic, exciting species of the galaxy, Time Pimp had chosen to mostly spend his time among and pimpin' humans. Pimps were distinctive in their dress, proud of their appearance and fiercely arrogant about their accomplishments, and deeply loved these traits when they were manifested in the human race.

So it pained him every time he saw these latex-covered mockeries of men and women, these aberrations without sexuality or self. The implications were numerous and awful. There was not a man or woman shuffling about the streets of lost Netzach who did not wear this oppressive costume. Even in the head-to-toe condom suits, they still seemed to fear contact with one another, as if thick, inflexible latex was still not enough to keep away the vile possibility of touch. Time Pimp expected a fight as he walked past them. He had scrapped with the likes of them before and felt there was no reason to think he wouldn't this time.

They parted straight away, as if knowing that what was just ahead would hurt him worse than they could with the latex-based weaponry built and concealed in their costumes. And in this, they were right. They didn't know about pleasure or connection, they knew nothing about the virtues of touch, but the people in condom armor were quite acutely familiar with how to inflict pain and what not to do with someone already in Perpetual Torment. Time Pimp looked up at a statue, a glowering, hate-filled evil statue in the city square of the capital of ruined, much-loved Netzach, Netzach whose sun was a woman of such beauty that she lit a planet, a woman Time Pimp had dreamed of making love to since had first looked up at her. And he knew therefore that the statue, the glowering hate-filled statue had done the opposite and had done the vile work that hung in the sky forever for him to see. Time Pimp, faced with this knowledge, faced with this world of no further possibilities ,could do more or less nothing at all but to let out a scream, a scream that vibrated his entire history.

Dante too was walking through the unspeakable. His experience of Perpetual Torment had been more recent, more authentic perhaps than what Time Pimp was going through. Perpetual Torment was right outside the building where he was strapped to the Perpetual Torment device. He had been angry at the Florentines because they were gluttonous, contentious, greedy and every other sin he could have named. He had in his heart felt separate from all things but the woman from whom Time Pimp had sought to liberate him. Time Pimp had brought him to Netzach so he could flee from grief and returned him to a city he had to grieve for.

When he had heard of Julissa the brick woman's plight and that of her world, he had been mortified. The concept of the noble human form made in God's image being reduced to brick and mortar was a sickening and pathetic one. He had briefly admitted into his imagination what it should look like if a city were built on people. And when he came back to the city he'd scorned because he loved it, he had seen glass trees of organs breeding corrals, unnecessary surgeries and a giant three-faced monster on a throne of human innards. In this place and for its conquerors, there was nothing noble about humanity and they had left no nobility in Florence.

He beheld on the streets of the lionheads' new Florence the act of love corrupted into the simplest, basest, cruelest variation, forced by lionheaded beasts at the threat of death to engage in sins of the flesh, to merge it without merging spirit. He had believed in love and hope, divinity and the glory of the human soul, and the lionheads deprived the world of this. Knowing forever that they were right outside and all he thought of God and love and art and hope and potential could be rendered false by ravenous invaders from another world. The Earth, his life, was gore and rape and degradation now and forever.

"I would destroy this brick by brick," he said to himself,

"but for the fact that I am one small man."

Time Pimp was once again a child. Sitting in a velvet lounge, surrounded by equally velvety ladies, some in fact with flesh that was head-to-toe velvet. He was a small boy, not quite tanned to perfection, his teeth still in his mouth, no hat upon his head to hide his purple pompadour, still his eyes were shaded for he was young, he still made pretense toward manhood. He was barefoot in his red velvet pajamas, his fingers tracing up and down the back of one of his beloved velvet nurse whores, not with lasciviousness or purpose but with a child's tenderness and curiosity. Another boy sat in the lounge as well, dressed in black velvet pajamas, his pompadour every bit as impressive as Time Pimp's, but his eyes, the pink of a white rabbit's, had no shades to conceal them.

A tall, magnificent man entered. He was appointed in forest-green velvet, his hat a good four feet high, his platform shoes a good six inches, making him stand over eleven feet high entered the velvet lounge. The nurse whores got on their knees, the velvetskinned one unzipping his velvet pants to pull out the rod of pulsing green orgone light inside them and taking it into her mouth. With two fingers, she splayed open her black velvet womanhood, revealing pink flesh inside and worked her clit as she sucked in the radiant pimphood. Time Pimp stared inside her in fascination and awe, wishing to know all there was to know about its secrets. The other boy's pink eyes were on the pimp himself. There was trepidation in them, since the man did not visit the boys often and it was not Cuntsmas or Take Your Lion to Work Day.

When the velvet lady climaxed, hitting paroxysms of love and staining the carpet with raspberry-scented juices, the godlike pimp moved down the line, giving each ho a taste in a manner that befit his station in life. His powerful hands were soft and giving as he ruffled their hair, his hips never thrusting outward, he was receptive and never tried to turn this ritual into a skullfuck. Time Pimp had spent his life admiring this and tried to replicate this self control, but always found himself thrusting a bit when he gaves his hos a taste. There was a smile on Time Pimp's young face as he learned the pimpish ways and got to know the insides and the scents of many women from many worlds and many times. A tear was falling from the other boy's face, which was turning almost the color of his eyes.

The pimp finished with the last of the hos and zipped himself up. He approached the crying pink-eyed boy and pulled back his hand. With less a slap than a flick of his wrist, he sent the pink-eyed boy flying into a cushioned, velvetlined wall.

"I will not take any crying," said the pimp, "a pimp don't raise no bitches. He pimps 'em!"

Not knowing any better, the young Time Pimp was laughing, though at the back of his consciousness trapped in Perpetual Torment, the older Time Pimp was fighting off being a bitch like the pink-eyed boy. Perpetual Torment was evolving, becoming the people he could never have in his life again. There was much he would have given to be right back there in that nursery and in spite of the other boy's bitchiness, to be kinder instead of laughing derisively. But he never would and the consequences of all that would happen on this day would dwell with him forever and sadly, would dwell with much of the universe as well.

Dante too was faced by that same grief. Confronted by the face of the one he would never see again, who he would never touch. He had written love poems to her pretending they were for other women and when they were together in public, he would try to cast his eyes away from her. But it had come to naught. She was only the face that haunted him, only the face of loss, the face of Perpetual Torment.

But it was a lovely face, a face that had brought him warmth in hope. A face that had led him to visions of angels and to a never-before-seen sense of wonder. Though he suffered knowing he would never lay hands upon her, that face even in the state of torment was doing something to him. Even in the pain of grief, he felt warmth. Even though his longing would be eternal and the world of the lionheads had replaced the one he had once loved where the one he had once loved once resided, he felt warm and right and wonderful.

A timestream away in the lionheads' Florence a puzzled lionhead technician suffered three angry glares from The Impatience.

"He is smiling! What kind of Perpetual Torment is this!"

"Forgive me, Impatience, I don't know why he does this. The function of the device is very straightforward and the pimp seems to indicate that the device works perfectly fine."

Again and again confronted by the face of the fair Beatrice, the face of the absent muse, Dante continued to smile and continued to be warm and joyful through grief and through suffering. His loss was ecstasy, his pain triumph. Again the woman he'd lost, the woman unhad, he was relaxing in his corpsechair, defying all that the lionheads knew of Perpetual Torment. Out of the corner of his eye, he spotted something unexpected something not right. There was a tentacle creeping towards him.

"Don't be afraid," said a voice in his head, "take my hand."

And in the place where suffering and bliss converged, the author of the Inferno grabbed hold of a phantom tentacle.

Time Pimp was still in the velvet lounge. The pink-eyed boy sat up, looking at the pimp who slapped him not with scorn but admiration.

"Boys, I got something to tell you," said the pimp, "I've talked to your uncle and the time has come…"

The pink-eyed boy stood up.

"No! You can't do this to us! It isn't right?"

Young Time Pimp cocked his head in the pink-eyed boy's direction.

"Can't do what? What's he going to do?"

The pink-eyed boy's face was all venom.

"He's doing it all for you. I don't get anything from this."

"You get to grow up!" the elder pimp snarled at the boy.

The boy crossed his arms.

"I don't want to! We can't grow up this fast!"

Little Time Pimp put his hand on his mouth.

"No! Already?"

The pimp knelt down, putting a hand on Time Pimp's head.

"Yes, Time Pimp. Every pimp must eventually abandon his children. And the time has come for me to do so."

"You and uncle are stupid!" cried the pink-eyed boy, "I'll hate you and Time Pimp forever!"

"I'll hate you and Time Pimp forever!"

"I'll hate you and Time Pimp forever!"

"I'll hate you and Time Pimp forever!"

Perpetual Suffering freeze-framed at this moment. It seemed to have reached the conclusion that this what the worst thing it could do to Time Pimp. It connected intimately with the broken Netzach, the two events bound together in causality and though the broken Netzach wounded him deep, the resounding loss from this moment in the velvet lounge hurt so very much more.

"I'll hate you and Time Pimp forever!"

"I'll hate you and Time Pimp forever!"

After what seemed like a century of the pink-eyed boy saying those words that would lead to what they led to and the possible lost Netzach there was something different. Being in the same frame of life for a good hundred years makes change quite noticeable, particularly when that change is a tentacle reaching toward you. Unlike Dante, who grasped the tentacle out of blind faith, Time Pimp knew what it was that was reaching for him and he welcomed it, because it meant Perpetual Suffering had not quite been achieved.

Dante and Time Pimp stood in a dark control room, lit only by the glow of a monitor which showed the two of them strapped to the human chairs in The Impatience's throne room. Somehow Time Pimp's orgone cane was in his hand. A very confused Dante could not keep his eyes off of the monitor.

"This device, is it showing us?" he asked.

"Yeah," said Time Pimp, "it is."

"How can it?" asked Dante, "we are standing here."

Time Pimp placed a hand on his chin.

"Well, maybe the Perpetual Torment and Suffering Device has a psychogenic control room, a place that exists psychically but not physically. And this is where the Torment and Suffering emanate from."

"So can we destroy it?" asked the poet.

"You sort of already did," Time Pimp replied, pointing at the monitor, which was focused on Dante's nearly beatific face, "it looks like you somehow managed to temporarily reverse it so that the octopi in my shoes could establish a telempathic link between us and bring us here. Your grief might end up saving us."

"I am grateful Signor Time Pimp. It's a shame we have only this world of monsters to return. I wish my grief could save the Earth as well."

Time Pimp and Dante, telempathically connected, heard whisperings coming from Time Pimp's shoes, the seeds of an idea. Dante could hear only whispers and a strange squeaking, but Time Pimp heard something else.

"Maybe we can," said Time Pimp, "there is a way."

"I will do anything."

Time Pimp frowned.

"That's good. I don't know if I wanna do this."

Dante took Time Pimp's hand.

"Signor Time Pimp, whatever must be done must be done and we have no choice in the matter."

"We have to go to this console and turn the machine up. I need to suffer at this moment harder and you need to reverse the orgone flow. We can create an orgone burst that makes the time stream itself eject the lionheads and repair existence."

Dante was surprisingly undeterred.

"Do you think that it will work?"

Time Pimp shrugged.

"I'm a pimp. I don't really know or care how time travel works."

The poet did something Time Pimp had yet to see him do, something that there had been little record or indication that he ever did—he laughed.

Time Pimp went to the console, fiddled with some switches and as he did contemplated what had made the poet able to experience grief and bliss at the same time the way he had. He had hated grief, and thus disdained the velvet lounge episode and all it had wrought more than anything. But the poet had suffered grief and came out smiling. There was something to be learned from all of this, though Time Pimp did not feel this was a time to learn.

And Time Pimp was back in the moment of grief. Time Pimp was hearing the pink-eyed child say he would hate him forever. The moment realer and more permanent and escape altogether impossible. The device had been turned up high enough that he lost the context of Perpetual Suffering, forgot in his state that he had ever known anything but this child's particular hatred and this pimp's particular loss. He almost forgot why it was tragic that this pimp was ready to leave him and why it saddened him that this child hated him so. His only clue that something may have been amiss about this mode of being was briefly overhearing "He's smiling, why is he smiling?"

And Dante was looking once more on the woman he could not be with and the face he would never see again. Losing and losing and losing. The device could find no greater suffering, but at the same time it was his highest joy and the world of suffering grew bright and the softness of a kiss he never had fell upon the poet's lips. In the worst of places, the worst of times, he still had that. He suddenly saw the monstrous frustrated faces of The Impatience each angry that Perpetual Torment could not harm the mortal, each angry that he was smiling.

And he saw as if through the monitor the light coming off him, the orgone light, channeled through Time Pimp's platforms touching the cane, powered by the Perpetual Torment device and the face of Beatrice and the dream of the best world imaginable. The time stream itself could feel the orgone burst, the explosion of pleasure and joy that came from love and longing and the triumph over perpetual torment. The time stream could feel it and it could suddenly feel that it had been invaded and poisoned and was inspired to seek better.

The Impatience's mouths let out a scream as it and all other things were briefly forced to conceive of the best of all possible worlds, the world of the face the poet longed for and of the joy in his heart that there was anything to long for at all.

Time Pimp, gone from the velvet lounge and back in the throne room, where he realized he had set the orgone cane from the wrong frequency to harm the lionheads. Inflicting pain would do no good since it was all they knew, it was pleasure, the kind of pleasure that could only come from defiance of the worst pain possible.

The orgone light and the light of the timestream made existence all go pink, like the inside of the tunnel to Netzach and feel as warm and sweet and welcoming as all of that. It was instantaneous and then all was clear. And Time Pimp and Dante stood on the bustling streets of Florence in the year 1290. The poet hugged the pimp, and the pimp allowed it.

"Signor Time Pimp, we have been through something beautiful. You wished me to get over my grief, so I could make my great work. And now I can. In the darkest of all places, in Perpetual Torment, the face of my lost love called out to me and told me about the best of all possible worlds. I can write now, about the soul's triumph over most anything. Thank you, Time Pimp. You have guided me through Hell and back."

"All in a day's work," said Time Pimp, beaming with pride, though pride he knew that he did not deserve.

The Purple Cadillac was parked right in front of them and Time Pimp got in. He drove to Netzach, looked up at the naked sun and behind his shades, he cried, he cried like a bitch but knew that it was proof of his strength. And though it hurt him, he sat down in the velvet lounge of his own whorehouse and for the first time in years, he thought long and hard about death.

# MURDER AT THE TIME CASINO

"You gonna do it?" asked Sister Cecilia.

"A pimp don't narc." Time Pimp took a whiff of his cognac, but didn't take a drink.

"A pimp also don't leave a client unsatisfied," she said solemnly, blue eyes burrowing into him.

"Why do you ask if I'm gonna do it? You know I'm gonna do it."

"I want to know if you know," she said, arms crossed, sweet pink mouth pursed.

"Course I know."

"You know he knows."

Time Pimp snickered.

"Does he?"

"I know he told you so."

Time Pimp was visibly upset.

"Don't play games with me, bitch! This isn't easy. You think I like knowing people are gonna hate me forever? This is bullshit. You two are gonna be loved forever. They won't even know who I am and they're gonna hate me."

She placed a hand on his shoulder and leaned in.

"You're gonna do something really noble. You're going to bring a lot of people hope and help a good man fulfill his purpose. And he is a good man, Playa. And you're a good man."

Time Pimp pushed her hand away.

"I don't care about noble. I'm a pimp. I gots to get paid and that's all."

She smiled. It was jarring for Time Pimp. Sister Cecilia rarely smiled. Her smile was awkward and weak. It looked like it pained her to make it happen. And yet, it made him feel a bit like the pink tunnel did. It made him feel like cold hard cash in his hand or a new piece of bling to power the Cadillac.

"But you are going to do the right thing. Believe it or not, you always do the right thing."

"He must make you feel real nice," said Time Pimp, tossing back his cognac. "I never seen you smile like that or talk sweet. That punk's gonna make you soft!"

Sister Cecilia hardened. She became the woman Time Pimp knew. The pale, flame-haired warriorwoman who brought men to their knees and often helped to keep his hos in line.

"What is this about?"

"I think you don't know who your pimp daddy is no more. I think he's got you convinced he's…"

"I'm not just any ho," she shot back, "don't treat me like I am. You're not acting like a pimp. You shouldn't need to prove anything."

"I did it all!" Time Pimp shouted, "I turned the water into wine, I got the loaves to breed, I brought the vaccine that cured Lazarus! I did it all and you're still acting like he ain't just some chump!"

"He paid you to do this job and you knew how important it was. He paid you for companionship in his last days. I did my job, Playa. You shouldn't bitch and sulk about doing yours!"

"Oh, I'll do it. And I'm gonna like it!" Time Pimp lied. He was going to do it. He had to do it. He had always done it. But he did not like it.

*14something, Objectively Later, The Steppes of Mongolia*

Cutlass clanged against Mongol scimitar. Boot met shin. Left hook pounded face. The nun was all of five foot three, but was more than a match for Genghis Khan, even if he was one of history's greatest warriors. She too was a superlative fighter. A fighter who could put her whole body into the battle, not deterred at all if her sword had been parried, seeing the man in front of her as a resource, each part of his body a new opportunity to inflict injury. Time Pimp was clutching the orgone cane perhaps too tightly. He hoped that she could not see him, for she would be insulted to know that the pimp was ready to back her up if things got out of hand.

Genghis Khan tried to follow her attack with an offhand punch of his own, but found his balance compromised as she gracefully swept his left leg. He didn't fall, but his grip on his scimitar wavered, his balance suffered and his stance widened just enough to send her knee into his groin.

"You're the dirty whore!" she screamed out, "you're the fucking filthy pain slut! I'm going to knock you down and I'm going to make you suck my fucking bootheel like a cock! You disgusting little slut!"

The Mongol only groaned in response. He had, after all, just been kneed violently in the groin. And then kicked in the ankle. And slapped in the face. And as he stumbled trying to regain his footing, been nicked in the face with the cutlass, marking him. He had a gash on his face, he was missing a tooth. He was emasculated and in excruciating pain. The groan was followed by panting and heavy breathing. As he got back his footing, he tried once again to go in for a slap. He was moving slower and perhaps deliberately so.

She caught his arm midstrike. Twisted it. There was a snap. His wrist went limp, hand bent backwards. She kicked his shin three times in rapid succession. Then the other shin. She marked his other cheek. The mighty Mongol warrior tried to remain on his feet, but could not. He hit the ground.

"Are you ready to surrender, whore?" Sister Cecilia snarled at him, "you weak, dickless pile of stinking horseshit! You're just a dirty little whore! You going to surrender?"

Genghis Khan tried to hide a smile as he shook his head "no." Sister Cecilia sat down on his chest.

"You think you're so fucking tough, huh? You're just a weak, dickless little whore. Bet you like dicks in your mouth so you can see what real men feel like!"

She sheathed the cutlass so both her hands were free for slapping. She added a red handprint to his recently marked face and then backhanded the other side. She quickly began to flow with it, thinking no longer of danger, but of her capacity for abuse and the healing power of the open palm. Hers was an errand of mercy through mercilessness, the lessons she imparted to the novices at the convent. She could hear nothing and think nothing but the sound of slapping and her next taunt.

"Genghis Cunt is more like it, you crusty gash! My cock's bigger than yours, you fucking pussy! Fill yourself with babies

41

and bake me a fucking pie! Put on a fucking apron and some sexy heels and mop up my fucking floor!"

She stood up, smashing the heel of her boot down on the Mongol's testicles. He cried, squealed, once again moaned. She did it again. Three more times. She spat on his face.

"I thought I was the whore, gashface. You ugly, stinking, weak puddle of cervical mucus! I should fist you to death you pathetic schoolgirl cumbucket!"

The warlord was hyperventilating. Although his testicles were being crushed, his penis was standing at attention. His oftslapped face was red not just from stinging and pain. The small but powerful siren whose pale skin and crimson bangs brought chills had him in a violently ecstatic state. If this were actually a duel, the winner would not be hard to determine. But, in these circumstances, Genghis Khan was pretty happy and actually doing quite well for himself. Even as Sister Cecilia shoved the heel of her other boot into his mouth, his body was quivering with joy.

"Suck it like you suck your horse's dick you horsefucking slut!" Her perfect visage serene and dispassionate, she vehemently facefucked one of the most dangerous men in human history. The Mongol warlord moaned into her boot, tears of joy running down his bloodstained, beaten cheeks until his body suddenly stopped squirming. He relaxed himself, closed his eyes and was free. Free from the harshness and violence of his barbarian childhood, free from the men he decapitated, the women he raped, the villages he'd burned. Free from authority. Violence given over to this angel became trustworthy and comforting. Violence became not violence but kindness. He had surrendered himself to a hired higher power, one in a tight leather nun's habit. And his goddess spoilt him with a bounty of sensuous beatings and the humbling degradation of a bootheel in his mouth.

She pulled out the bootheel and helped the Mongol to his feet. He opened his eyes again and was clearly very much at ease. Sister Cecilia planted a chaste kiss upon his cheek and said a quiet benediction. She laughed, a laugh that tickled like an errant hair brushing across his face. He laughed too but did not understand why. She had learned to laugh this way and to elicit these laughs from someone dear to her. Few people were dear to her, so she carried their lessons close and made good use of them. He gave her a deep bow, which she returned.

Genghis Khan took the rein of his horse and handed it to Sister Cecilia. She was confused at first, but in a few seconds figured it out. She nodded her approval. And at that, Genghis Khan walked off. Time Pimp mumbled something incredibly obscene. The obscenities of Netzach were among the finest in the universe. Sister Cecilia stroked the horse's mane.

"Well, Playa, you can slap me around if you like, but I'm not giving you 30 percent of this horse."

Time Pimp laughed in spite of himself.

"You can keep it. It's your birthday."

Sister Cecilia closed one eye and tilted her head, thinking about it.

"Was when you came to get me. Guess it is. I don't really know how time travel works. Or care."

"Nobody does."

"But if you can go to any point in time, why did you choose to come see me on my birthday?"

Time Pimp shrugged.

"Why not? You're one of my top earnin' bitches."

She shook her head.

"No, something's up with you. Something happened. You barely came round to check on me after the whole Magdalene thing. Now you go pick me up on my birthday."

Time Pimp pulled out a shotglass, spat into it, turned his spit into cognac and drank it.

"I ain't gotta explain myself to no bitches."

She looked him over, but not for long. She decided her new horse was more interesting than a strangely sentimental pimp. But not as interesting as the sudden musky feminine scent in the air. A timewomb was opening. Time Pimp clutched the orgone cane and Sister Cecilia grabbed her cutlass off the ground. They had not met other time travelers they were fond of, and there was always one in particular that they were on the lookout for.

The pink concentric circles of energy appeared and out of them stepped a panda in a labcoat. He was wearing gigantic goggles that made sounds like the shutter of a camera. He looked a consummate mad scientist, save for his baggy pale pink sweatpants that read "Daddy's Girl." He spoke, his voice refined, his enunciation perfect.

"Greetings, Time Pimp of Netzach, Sister Cecilia of Anhedonia…"

"Geburah," Sister Cecilia corrected the panda. Cold, hard, matter of fact.

The panda placed his hand over his mouth.

"Oh, my, I am terribly sorry for the oversight, Sister. Pardon me."

"It's all right," she said, in a tone one does not use to say that things are all right. There was a heavy, awkward silence before the panda spoke up again.

"I, most esteemed chrononauts, am Professor Panda. I come from Fank Toblerone, the googleplexionaire. He wishes to invite you both to the grand opening of The Time Casino. We have invited historical figures from all over the stream to come and gamble and have fun at the most exciting place in spacetime, conveniently situated at the end of time."

Time Pimp placed his hand on his chin.

"Hmm, sounds like the perfect way to celebrate this bitch's birthday. Fank's an old friend of mine. Motherfucker knows how to party."

Professor Panda nodded emphatically.

"Why, certainly, Mister Time Pimp, sir! I could not be more firmly in agreement. There is plenty to do, though we have come to you in part for business reasons. We're looking for you to provide…"

The panda blushed, his fur turning the color of his very effeminate sweatpants.

"Some of the entertainment."

"Sounds profitable. You got yoselves a pimp, Mister Panda."

Professor Panda crossed his arms and put his adorable nose up in the air.

"Professor. I didn't go to the time travel academy to be called Mister."

"You got yoselves a pimp, Mister Panda."

The panda had heard enough about Time Pimp not to press the issue further. He reached into his pocket and pulled out a sheet of paper.

"Here are the temporal coordinates for the end of time."

Time Pimp took them and the panda vanished into another timewomb.

"Hmm," said Sister Cecilia, "this might prove interesting."

"I'm sure it will. Fank is the richest man of all time. We're gonna spend your birthday in style, bitch."

They loaded Sister Cecilia's new horse into the Purple Cadillac and took off for Netzach, where they dropped him off to coos of pleasure and excitement and picked up a car full of hos, which in the case of the Purple Cadillac was somehow a hundred hos. With a push of a button, the back seat of the Purple Cadillac expanded, transforming into a gigantic hot tub about the size of an Olympic swimming pool. The Purple Cadillac had gone from an automobile to a purple pimping stretch limousine of pure sensuality. Bodies of all shapes and sizes from across millennia and galaxies disrobed. Naked mantiswomen, naked cavegirls, naked catgirls, naked Viking girls, naked flappers, naked hermaphrodites, naked cyborgs, naked geishas, naked Egyptian slave girls, naked weresharks, naked cowgirls.

They tossed beachballs back and forth. They kissed and fondled each other, unaware of race or planet or time of origin and not caring. Catgirl gleefully bit down on mantistit. Viking shieldmaiden giggled as a sharkwoman swam up beneath her to tenderly tongue her anus. Whitechapel whores took the fat cocks of hermaphroditic punk girls of the 27th Century into their mouths, rouged cheeks bulging with the future of fucking. Leather nuns of Geburah, the novices of Sister Cecilia's convent practiced their spanking skills on the bionic buttocks of cybernetic pleasure soldiers. The scent of the hot tub and the scent of the timewomb intermingled and it was barely distinguishable where one ended and the other began.

Pale, dark, green, brown, yellow, ebony, brick…there was only flesh and passion in the Purple Cadillac.

But this was commonplace for Time Pimp's Purple Cadillac. Him and Sister Cecilia sitting in the front of the car did not even feel inclined to look backwards. They were instead focused on the pink tunnel, minds full of anticipation and curiosity about what the end of time would be like and what the richest man of all time would do with his money. The Time Casino was an intriguing proposition, if it was indeed the crowning achievement of the man who has everything.

They had expected the Time Casino to be in orbit or on the surface of a planet at the end of time. Perhaps for it to be an entire planet by itself. But the truth of the matter was even more exciting and perplexing. When the Purple Cadillac came to a stop at the End of Time, the car was beside a giant fountain that projected molten gold into the air, sitting on the surface of a red carpet made of monomolecular rubies. Professor Panda was waiting with an army of luminescent beings that were telekinetically floating trays of drinks around their hyperevolved bodies. The trays emptied of drinks, each immediately appearing in the hands of Time Pimp, Sister Cecilia and the hos who were emerging perfectly dry and fully clothed from The Purple Cadillac. They did not need to land anywhere or enter a building because the Time Casino was the only thing to exist at The End of Time.

"I trust," said Professor Panda, "that your journey was a good one."

"A pimp never has a bad trip. A pimp travels in style."

Professor Panda nodded.

"Indeed. None could dispute that, Playa."

"So where's your bossman at, Mister Panda?"

Ten of the energy beings vanished and in each of their place, there stood a smooth, perfectly toned bald young man of about nineteen. Upon looking at these ten young men, each of the hos squirted with pleasure onto the monomolecular ruby carpet, such was his perfection. Sister Cecilia had to breathe and clench herself to avoid doing as the hos had, even Time Pimp was clutching the orgone cane to reduce his pleasure level. Fank Toblerone had bought himself the best body he could comprehend and then hired someone better at comprehending bodies to come up with a better one. Ten of them. He was a testament to the pimp race's belief that money could do absolutely anything.

"Time Pimp, hos," said the ten young men all at once, "welcome to The Time Casino, the greatest place of all time at the last and greatest time of all time. I thank you for bringing with you the finest ladies of all time. My guests are going to be very demanding."

Time Pimp leaned back on a holocolumn. He was trying to seem unimpressed by the splendor of the casino lobby.

"How demanding?"

"Well," said all ten of the richest man of all time, "they are the best people in history. Some of them might already be on your client list but many aren't, Time Pimp. Even a pimp will be quite amazed by the casino's splendors and its guests."

A pterodactyl landed beside the rich man. A confident looking Victorian gentleman dressed in a dashing coat accompanied by a deerstalker hat was riding on its back. He had a pipe in his mouth. Time Pimp couldn't help but smile wide. Sister Cecilia did the same. It had been some time since they had seen the famed Englishman, the consulting detective. He approached the pimp, extending his hand.

"Time Pimp."

Time Pimp felt like embracing his old friend, but knew that this was not a man who was particularly into public displays of affection or into being touched at all except under the right circumstances, which were extraordinarily specific and by some people's standards quite perverse—hell, even by Time Pimp's standards, they were quite perverse, to the point at which the detective's sexuality looked nothing like sexuality at all. His relationship with Watson was far more vanilla than his other proclivities.

"My main man Sherlock Holmes! It is once again an honor to see you. How's Watson these days?"

Holmes raised an eyebrow.

"How's Watson at the end of time? I imagine he's not

particularly well, Time Pimp."

Time Pimp had to think about that one for a second. Not knowing or caring how time travel worked, Time Pimp had a great deal of difficulty deciding whether or not to try and clarify the statement.

"I suppose he wouldn't be. Just makin' small talk, Sherlock. It's good to see you again my friend."

"Likewise, my dear Time Pimp, likewise."

He approached Sister Cecilia and bowed. She offered her hand to kiss.

"Sister. How old are you today? Or rather on the day Time Pimp picked you up."

"Well, you know, Sherlock, a lady never reveals her age, but I am impressed that you picked up that it was my birthday."

"Yes, well, I am Sherlock Holmes after all." Sherlock Holmes turned around as gauchely as he was expected to, mounting the pterodactyl again and flying off.

A small time womb opened and out stepped a thin, bald, familiar-looking Indian man. Though Time Pimp recognized the gentleman, they had not yet met in person. The Indian man bowed.

"Namaste. I have been told you are the finest pimp in the history of pimping. I look forward to sampling your wares."

"I look forward to serving you, Mister Gandhi. It is most certainly an honor."

Fank Toblerone smiled arrogantly with all ten of his chiseled faces.

"You see, Time Pimp? I cater to only the finest people in history. Greatness is a strain so I have called them here for a temporary respite to be a secret participant in their greatness. History flourishes thanks to Fank Toblerone."

Professor Panda cleared his throat loudly.

"And to you, Professor Panda. I chose my science advisor well. You are perhaps the only person in history who actually knows how time travel works."

Time Pimp and Sister Cecilia were both quite shocked. Neither of them had the slightest idea how time travel worked and although Time Pimp did not care it was impressive that somebody had in fact figured it out. He had to wonder if the Purple Cadillac had worked this whole time thanks to Professor Panda's research, making the panda an accomplice to every magnificent act of time travel that had ever occurred, a secret saviour of history greater than Time Pimp himself. He didn't think about that for long as the thought grew confusing and boring since there was no way of figuring out whether it was possible for Professor Panda to have done that. Sister Cecilia, however, was quite intrigued.

"Could you explain time travel to me? I've always wondered about it."

The panda placed both his warm, furry, black paws over Cecilia's hand, he pulled up his goggles revealing big, brown, sincere, tender eyes.

"Sister, you make a panda so happy for asking. I find most time travelers do not care how time travel works as well as not knowing and find the very thought of someone explaining it quite tiresome indeed. But, yes, I should like very much to teach you the inner workings of chronotravel even down to the exact workings of Time Pimp's Purple Cadillac and the origins of the timewombs. Origins that are quite shocking and interesting."

"I'm sure they are." She planted a small kiss on Professor Panda's face.

The panda blushed pink again.

Time Pimp found himself a bit jealous. He remembered when he had met Sister Cecilia on Anhedonia. He remembered the abuses she had endured at the convent. He remembered the suffering of the people of Anhedonia as the Morality Front was enacting the hundred-year occupation plan. He remembered the blank, joyless stare on her face as he yanked her by the arm into the Purple Cadillac, wondering why his shoes had brought him to such a frigid bitch. He remembered her steadfast refusal to leave and how she made him do the right thing and go back to teach the other nuns pleasure even as they risked the wrath of the Morality Front. He remembered her raising the pirate cutlass and decapitating the abbess. He remembered her standing on the abbess' balcony screaming "GEBURAH!" and the screams of Geburah below. He remembered how he hated her for the attention she was bringing to him and for making him lead a revolution though a pimp doesn't stick his neck out for no bitches. He thought back on her thorough but joyless whippings of clients and her refusal of the delights of Netzach. And how the client had brought her happiness when he could not, though he had done all the work and there was nothing special about that loser. She smiled and laughed all the time. She had kissed a panda. He resented the happier Sister Cecilia.

"Enough wastin' time with this chump, lets go have some fun and get ourselves paid!"

"By all means," said all ten of Fank Toblerone, "by all means. All of the columns and walls have psychoreactive displays, even the one you're leaning on. They will scan your mind for activities you may enjoy and suggest them back to you. If you are seeking novelty, they will implant new ones. Only, however if you are seeking novelty."

Sister Cecilia pushed Time Pimp aside slightly, placing her hand on the column. She bounced up and down joyfully, a sight that reminded Time Pimp just how tight her leather habit was, able to keep her ample breasts from bouncing at all.

"Intertemporal gladiator games! This is going to be great!"

Time Pimp placed his hand on the column, which flooded his psyche with the idea that Intertemporal gladiator games would indeed be great. He was hoping the column would offer him something more refined, being the man of distinction that he was, but the column had decided Sister Cecilia was calling the shots, possibly acknowledging that it was her birthday and this was therefore due to her. Before he could ask how the column worked, he and Sister Cecilia were seated on a giant, furry, pink couch. Edgar Allan Poe was seated beside them, enjoying a glass of port. They seemed to be in a kind of existential bubble outside an arena cordoned off by a forcefield.

The floor of the arena was icy, and sharp axes were swinging above the heads of the two combatants, one of them an ancient Roman armed with a trident and net, the other a gigantic robot kangaroo swinging a huge spiked club. The kangaroo was screaming things out in French. On branches extending from the arena's invisible walls, genetically engineered vultures played checkers with their beaks, their eyes occasionally wandering dispassionately to the gladiator/ kangaroo battle, no doubt to see if the time had come to clean up. Smooth jazz played from a miniature blimp circling the conflict. Yet somehow all Time Pimp could bring himself to think was "Damn, this shit looks expensive."

One of the light beings shimmered into existence, handed Time Pimp and Cecilia drinks, then shimmered back out of being. They quietly toasted each other and clinked glasses with Poe, whose eyes finally left the battle.

"I was told about you, sir," said the writer, "you're that Time Pimp, aren't you?"

"That I am. And this here's Sister Cecilia. Leather nun extraordinaire. Trains all my leather nuns."

"I'm a big fan of yours," said Sister Cecilia to Poe, "I love a good murder."

"As do I," said Poe, returning his eyes to the gladiator and the kangaroo. The axes were descending and the kangaroo was bearing down on the Roman.

"Je voudrais un croque monsieur!"

The kangaroo brought down the club, but the Roman rolled out of the way, tossing his net at the robotic beast's head. As the kangaroo got distracted, the Roman crawled between its legs, thrusting up with the trident at where the crotch would be on most beings. It took three thrusts, but the kangaroo's crotch let loose a series of sparks. The beast wobbled.

"Je voudrais un croque monsieur!" it screamed out in pain.

"It wants a sandwich," Poe explained.

The gladiator rolled out from the kangaroo's legs. He stood up, now directly behind the robotic marsupial. As he searched the animal's metallic back for a weakness, he failed to see that a smaller roboroo was emerging from the kangaroo's marsupial pouch, It was carrying a small laser pistol and its eyes were glowing with malice. The gladiator did indeed find a weak spot in the robot kangaroo's backplate and shoved the trident into it deep, letting loose another rain of sparks.

"Pourquois?" the kangaroo shrieked, "Je t'adore!"

The kangaroo bent down, no longer operational and the Roman faced the audience to give a bow. Sadly, he had still failed to notice the mechanical joey now pointing a laser gun at him. The laser pistol let out a pulse of blue energy, made a humming noise and before the gladiator could even turn around to see the source of the sound, his body was smoking and sizzling and he was dead.

"Excellent sport," said Poe to Sister Cecilia, "but not particularly sporting."

"Well, you can hardly fault the kangaroos for having more advanced technology."

"No," said Poe, suddenly afflicted by melancholy, "I suppose we cannot. This might seem unnatural to me, but it is still nature and nature is quite cruel."

Time Pimp was growing quite tired of the melancholy of writers. He hoped the next historical figure they met would be neither a writer nor melancholy. He touched the column without so much as saying goodbye to Poe. He did not much need Poe's approval. He found himself drawn toward a lounge. He liked lounges. There was generally no place more suitable for a pimp than the lounge. He had been to and had set up many fine lounges and took great pleasure in sitting, having a drink and chatting up some fine ladies from history.

Of all the temporal gin joints and all the casinos in all of time, she had to walk into this one. A distant-eyed strawberry blonde patrician whose skirt showed pride in her legs and whose sweater was just tight enough to draw a man's attention was sulking over a glass of red wine. Time Pimp couldn't help but wonder whether she had known he would be here and why, if she'd known, she had taken up Professor Panda and Fank Toblerone's offer. Of all the temporal gin joints and all the casinos in all of time, Sylvia Plath had to walk into this one. He had had a hard time with Dante, he had had a hard time thinking of the happier, brighter, sweeter Sister Cecilia but those hard times were a cakewalk compared to the heartbreak the poetess represented.

He tried to shift his attention to the quantum slot machines or to the fencing trapezists swinging overhead. Thing is, Time Pimp was a pimp. A man in a red velvet suit wearing a flamboyant purple hat, shades and platform shoes in which psychic octopi floated in absinthe. He was the opposite of anyone's definition of discreet.

"Are you going to come over and say hello, Playa, or shall I just stare into my drink and think of you as you were?" Her speech was slightly slurred. This was not her first glass of this wine nor would it likely be her last.

"No," said Time Pimp.

"Then I will stare into my drink," she said, "and think of you as you were, which is a travesty because there you are."

He raised his glass.

"That's life, pretty lady."

He fought against the urge to see the two of them once more in the back seat of The Purple Cadillac, parked on a cliff overlooking the absinthe sea of Netzach where love and death and rebirth were one, the most special place he could ever show a woman, filling her with the radiance of his big, big pimpin', an experience not soured in the least by knowing her macabre and melancholy history. And she thought not about her husband and her children and her death but only of the pimp she loved and the time she had spent in his stable of hos, learning to perfect the arts of love. And perfect she had. Time Pimp took few lovers and usually did not give the cock to his hos at all, but Sylvia was one of a kind. Sylvia was…

He tried to search his mind for memories from all over history, to flood his brain with his adventures, but he could not. He was haunted by the absinthe sea and the moment of Eros and Thanatos together taking in Netzach's perfection and Sylvia's perfection. Plath would later write that she had been perfected and when she did, she would be remembering and referring to this time spent making love in a Purple Cadillac above the ocean where pimps went to become octopi for the magic platform shoes of future pimps. And every time Time Pimp heard the words he would remember this place and this time with this fine, fine lady.

53

She sat down at his table. She stared at him that way she stared at things. It could have been schizoid distance or deathliness or fascination but it didn't matter. She got transfixed easily, and it did something to his heart and to the energy in his pants. She placed her arm on his. He wanted to pull away but he could not. Strawhatted jazzbots seemed to be emerging from the floor to play Saint James Infirmary Blues. Let her go, God bless her...

And they were dancing. And Christmas-bulb fireflies were circling their heads. And the dancefloor levitated away from the bar, letting them float one-hundred feet above the ground with the jazzbots playing the eternal dirge for the both of them. He had never been morbid, he had always tried to avoid letting death cross his mind, but this moment was rare and exquisite nonetheless and this woman...

An energy being blinked in, leaving Time Pimp with a tray of Netzach absinthe, the stuff in his shoes wherein floated the two octopi, reminders that even a Time Pimp had to eventually relinquish his life and move onto the next step. It was a cruel reminder of this, but the burn and the anise and the gyres in his head made it all worthwhile. Of all the Time Casinos in all the world, Sylvia Plath had to walk into his and to make him feel this way again to make him feel stupid feelings like a bitch. She was his ho was and it was still within his right to slap her, but he could not bring himself to do so.

He was grateful for the pretty, dark-haired woman who tapped him on the shoulder. Tall, slender, dressed in a tight, black cocktail dress, she proved herself the perfect femme fatale when she spoke, revealing a Russian accent.

"May I have the next dance?"

He knew he had seen her somewhere, but he could not quite place her face. Perhaps she was more dressed up than he usually saw her, wherever he had seen her before.

"You sure can, bitch," he said, "you got the skills to pay the bills."

"Hrrumph," Sylvia hrrumphed.

The jazzbots switched over to Minnie the Moocher.

"I gotta admit," said Time Pimp, "I know I've seen you

somewhere, but I can't place the face."

The woman pulled away, slapping Time Pimp in the face. "You are rotten bastard!" she screamed, "I am Ayn Rand! You will never forget my name!"

Placing her hand on a nearby column, she vanished. Time Pimp was disappointed. As a pimp, many aspects of her work had appealed to him. And she seemed pretty hot to trot. She certainly practiced what she preached when it came to ego. Time Pimp walked away from Sylvia, placing his hand on a column and thinking of business, somewhere where he could get in touch with more of his potential clients.

The column sent him to the bleachers at a shark race. Seated beside him was a tall, blonde-haired man dressed in a Hawaiian shirt and shorts whose eyes were a mile wide at the sight of the dwarves on sharkback.

"Holy shit," said the blonde man, "this is the best thing ever."

Those words indicated to Time Pimp that he was sitting beside a great author and zen master who was spoken of often at pimp school. In 2026, this man had ruled the Earth for 11 minutes before remembering that he had found politics boring and going off to do something awesome.

"It's not bad," Time Pimp replied.

"No!" said a familiar voice, "You have got to be fucking kidding me!"

Two rows down, Sister Cecilia was arguing with an old Chinese man. Time Pimp walked down to join them. Cecilia gave Time Pimp a one-handed wave hello. The old Chinese man stood up and gave Time Pimp a deep bow.

"You must be the one with the hos," said the Chinese man, "I am Lao Tzu."

"Wow," said Time Pimp, "I love *The Art of War*."

"Naah, it's a different guy," said Sister Cecilia, "I think that was Sun Tzu."

"I am here for the hos," said Lao Tzu.

"Nice to meet you," said Time Pimp.

"TIME PIMP!" a black-haired man in the natty dress of an early nineteenth-century aristocrat shouted as he descended the bleachers with a pronounced limp, "I should have known I'd find you here, you rascal!"

Sister Cecilia's pale skin blanched whiter.

"Oh no…"

"And Sister Cecilia!" he embraced the leather nun tightly, not missing an inappropriate opportunity to grope her small, tight ass.

"Please don't touch me."

The fop laughed boisterously.

"Same old Cecilia! It's so nice to see the two of you again!"

"Yes," said Time Pimp, not trying at all to feign excitement, "it's great to see you again, Lord Byron."

"I'm so glad you feel that way. I should have known it would be so. After all, what's a few million pounds between friends?"

"A few million pounds," grumbled Time Pimp.

"I look forward to seeing what kind of girls you've brought for the entertainments here. I'm certain you've outdone yourself."

Time Pimp and Sister Cecilia went to great effort to stifle their urge to beat the living shit out of the famed Romantic poet. They just barely succeeded at this. Byron owed Time Pimp a great deal of money and had a tendency to leave the girls he made use of barely in working order by the time he was done with them. Time Pimp had sworn if their paths ever crossed again he would inflict a great deal of pain on the scoundrel, but was in an awkward position, Byron also being a guest of Fank Toblerone as he was.

Time Pimp's request for the column to bring him to historical clients had proven quite effective, but he was not getting what he bargained for. The two men who next descended the bleachers proved this. One of them was a small wild-eyed man wearing a purple pinstriped suit and beside him was a blonde-haired blue-eyed cowboy dressed all in black. The purple pinstriped man ran up to Byron giving him a big hug and kissing him on both cheeks.

"I rather like the fashions of this time," said the purple pinstriped suit man, "much better than the togas. I never much liked the togas. It is good to see you again, Lord Byron. I am tempted to spare your life."

"That would be very kind of you," said Byron returning the man's kisses on the cheek, "who's your friend?"

The cowboy tipped his hat.

"Jesse James at your service."

The purple pinstriped man broke his embrace to extend his hand to Time Pimp. He did so palm down to present a massive ruby ring.

"Emperor Caius Caligula. You may kiss my ring."

"I don't think I will."

The Roman emperor turned to Byron.

"Is this the Time Pimp you were talking about?"

"The very same."

"Time Pimp," said Time Pimp, "pleased to meet you, Caligula."

Caligula wept softly.

"Nobody ever says that to me."

"I don't like Romans," said Sister Cecilia, "maybe people would be pleased to meet you if you didn't kill them so much."

"How much to let me kill her?" asked Caligula, pulling out a Hello Kitty wallet.

Time Pimp clutched the orgone cane tight. Caligula shrugged and put back his wallet.

"Suit yourself. How does one become a Time Pimp? I think I might like it."

A group of dignified old ladies dressed in Tam O' Shanter hats came down for a brief moment.

"Time Pimp, on behalf of the Wealthy Dowager's Supper Club of Binah, it is wonderful to see you again."

"Wonderful to see you again too," said Time Pimp, trying to be polite even though he had never liked the Wealthy Dowager's Supper Club.

"Who is your handsome friend?" said a wealthy dowager with a big smile on her face. She was indicating Caligula.

"Caius Caligula," said the Roman emperor, "and I'm going to make sweet love to your lungs."

The Supper Club fainted in unison. Time Pimp would have

made some effort to rouse the old ladies were it not for the sudden arrival of Professor Panda through a small timewomb.

"You all must come with me!" he insisted.

There was a luxurious sitting room waiting for them. The historical personages had already sat down in big comfortable armchairs. There were two others, one with a placard declaring it Time Pimp's spot, the other one labeled "Sister Cecilia." Time Pimp and Cecilia sat down begrudgingly but did not feel good about it. Caligula. Ayn Rand. Edgar Allan Poe. Sylvia Plath. Gandhi. Sherlock Holmes. Jesse James. Lao Tzu. Professor Panda. Lord Byron. All of these guests had been brought together into a locked room that felt very much like a trap. Time Pimp was already trying to think away to force his way out, or to get Toblerone to unlock the sitting room. Perhaps he could douse the fire in the giant fireplace against the wall and escape out through the chimney somehow.

Just then Fank Toblerone walked in through the fireplace, eliminating this possibility by revealing the fireplace to be nothing but a rare heat projecting hologram. At least that made the fake wall an escape possibility.

"What's this about?" shouted an impatient Lord Byron, smashing his glass on the floor histrionically.

"Yes!" screamed Caligula grabbing a shard from Byron's glass and cutting his face with it.

"I too am impatient!" he broke into a maniacal cackle.

Byron, not one to be outdone began to cackle maniacally himself.

"I agree with these madmen," said Poe. "This is highly unorthodox, sir! Inviting someone as a guest and then locking them in a sitting room makes you a very poor host, sir!"

"I am here for the hos," Lao Tzu proclaimed, "If you wish to detain me, then bring me hos."

"Yes!" said Byron, "If we are to be subjected to imprisonment in a sitting room, the least you could have done is have Time Pimp send hos to the place!"

Professor Panda stood, holding out a paw.

"Now, now, I know you gentlemen are impatient, but Mister Toblerone brought you here to do some business.

When it is done, I am certain there will be plenty of time to spend with hos."

"I certainly hope so," said Gandhi, "It is rude to promise hos and then keep us away from the hos. Even my patience is tried."

"Perhaps," said Sherlock Holmes, "You should let the man speak his peace, so we can get out of this sitting room and get on to the pleasures of the flesh."

Ayn Rand put her feet up on Caligula's lap, toying with his crotch with a high-heeled foot.

"There is no reason the pleasures of the flesh can't be found in this sitting room."

"Maybe," said Sylvia, "Holmes is right and we should listen to our host so that we can find out what is actually going on."

"Yes," replied Professor Panda, nodding emphatically. "We should be quiet so that our host can speak. He does have important business to execute with you."

"Yes," said all of Fank Toblerone, "I have gathered you here for a reason."

The historical figures mumbled something akin to "you'd better have."

"I have gathered you here," said all ten of Fank Toblerone, "not because you are heroes and geniuses. I have gathered you here because one of you is a murderer."

Caligula giggled like a schoolgirl.

"Is that all? Yes, I've murdered thousands. I will murder more of you. I am a hateful god. And I punish mortals at my leisure. You cannot stop me from doing this."

"That was a duel!" shouted Byron shaking his fist.

"I believe," said Sherlock Holmes, lighting his calabash, "that for a man as wealthy as Mr. Toblerone, the only significant murder would be his own. Fank Toblerone has gathered us together in The Time Casino to unmask and punish his murderer, who could be any of us. Though is most likely not Miss Rand as she could never bring herself to murder a man as rich as Fank Toblerone."

"Yes," said Rand, leaning toward Toblerone to expose her

cleavage, "he is the finest specimen of mankind I have ever seen."

Caligula gasped.

"But you told me…"

Rand huffed.

"I'd have done anything to get you into bed. Your contempt for lesser beings makes you an ideal lover. But your mental illness makes you a lesser being than Mister Toblerone. Who is more powerful than the ten richest people in the world?"

"The Council of Fank Toblerone concurs," said Fank Toblerone, deciding that he was a council, which he had been the entire time.

Sherlock Holmes loudly cleared his throat.

"If I may…"

"Yes," said an excited Professor Panda, "Please continue! I am a huge fan."

"I don't care," said the great detective, "I was talking about solving a mystery. Which I will dazzle you all by doing before Mister Toblerone unmasks the killer. It will be my greatest triumph! Solving a murder that hasn't even happened yet!"

All present applauded. Ayn Rand fell to her knees and pulled up her skirt, presenting herself like a cat to Toblerone. All ten of Toblerone talked among themselves. Rand had been a big hero of theirs. And there was also the notion of being preempted by Sherlock Holmes before he could unmask his killer.

"Please continue, Holmes," said Toblerone, "and Miss Rand, your offer of anal sex with all ten of us is accepted. I will call for a surgical bot so we can expand your anal cavity big enough to take it."

Rand cackled with pleasure at her impending superiority. She salivated with glee at the prospect of having the single most expansive, formidable anus of all time. This would make her a goddess on Earth, a truly unstoppable force for genius.

"Ooh, yes," she said, "make me a goddess!"

Lao Tzu smiled, quite amused.

"By solving your murder, you murder yourself. Don't you understand?"

"I believe," said Sherlock Holmes, "that I was about to unmask Fank Toblerone's murderer."

"I just did," said the Chinese philosopher, "Fank Toblerone's murderer is Fank Toblerone. If he hadn't called us here, he would never be in the same locked room with his murderer. Fank Toblerone murdered himself. Murder solved. I will pleasure prostitutes now."

Lao Tzu turned to leave but was stopped by the sound of a pistol's click. Holmes was pointing a pistol at him.

"You remain a suspect. You do not get to leave. So get back here."

Lao Tzu turned back around with a shrug and sat back down in his chair.

"You are as arrogant as you are perverse, Sherlock Holmes."

"Let's all just be quiet so we can hear what Sherlock Holmes has to say," said Professor Panda.

The historical figures mumbled dissent but then quieted down.

Holmes cleared his throat and began to explain.

"Mr. Toblerone is…"

The room went completely dark and silent. Time Pimp was not pleased by this because he knew what it had to be. There were a series of productive voids in the Time Casino, capable of isolating reality and keeping one part of the Time Casino from interfering with another. A localized void would make the room completely dark and silent for a moment and the one who used the device would be able to do as they pleased in the dark and be both invisible and inaudible. This would have seemed like the work of a high-tech criminal had Time Pimp not known that void generators were as easy as pushing a button on a detonator, so even a person not used to modern technologies could pick such a thing up easily enough. Anyone could use it and anyone could do whatever they wanted to in the dark.

The void faded and light returned to the room. There were ten corpses on the ground and all of them were Fank Toblerone. He had been strangled with a rope, beaten with a candlestick, stabbed with a bloody knife that was in Caligula's hand, bashed with a lead pipe that Byron was holding, shot in the back, had his face caved in with a wrench that was sitting at Professor Panda's feet, poisoned, somehow thrown down from an extremely high elevation, and frightened to death. Fank Toblerone had somehow been murdered ten times in a very short duration and, like he had implied before his death, one of the killers had to be in the room. All eyes went straight to Caligula.

"I only stabbed the one," the mad Caesar insisted, "I swear!"

"I believe you," said Sherlock Holmes, "a man as completely mad as yourself would never commit a murder without bragging about it."

"I picked up this lead pipe because it was on the ground and I thought it would be nice to own a lead pipe," Byron explained.

"Yes," said Holmes, "it is a lovely pipe, yet I still find your story as they say colloquially in this time 'hard to swallow.'"

"Sir, you're in the wrong," said Byron, "I'm quite easy on the throat." He gave Sister Cecilia a lascivious wink.

"You know that's quite improper," said Sylvia, wagging a finger, "a man just died."

"Yeah," said Time Pimp, "the rich motherfucker who was going to pay me for my hos."

"Not problem," said Lao Tzu, "we will find money. I am here for whores. We should go to the hot tub and have an orgy."

Byron clapped the Chinese philosopher on the back, "Yes, capital idea! I've always enjoyed your work. I do exactly what my instincts tell me and my instincts tell me to have a hot tub orgy."

Caligula bounced up and down in place.

"Orgy orgy orgy orgy orgy…"

"You're speaking my language partner," said the thus far laconic Jesse James, "I reckon we could all make use of a good whore."

"Now, hold on…" Time Pimp started, but was interrupted when the lights went out once again. A shot rang out. Almost everyone screamed. Time Pimp could deduce that Lao Tzu and Holmes had kept calm and the source of the wicked laughter that had followed the screaming could only be Caligula. When the lights came back on, there was one less historical personality since somebody had shot Jesse James in the back. To everyone's surprise, Caligula, while almost doubled over with laughter, was not holding the gun at all.

"We're all going to die!" screamed Gandhi.

"We are already dead," said Lao Tzu, "this is the end of time."

"I think it might be best that we get out of this room and into some place where everyone's actions are transparent and where we are no longer locked in," said Holmes.

"Everyone is naked in a hot tub," argued Lao Tzu, "and we did all come here for whores."

"I suppose," said Time Pimp, "given that another man just died, I might be a little flexible on payment, but you bitches will find me my money or you will know the back of my hand."

Lao Tzu bowed deeply.

"This is casino. There is money everywhere."

"Yes!" cried Byron, "Fantastic idea! We fuck whores then we gamble."

"Orgy! Orgy! Orgy!"

Professor Panda searched around Toblerone's desk and found a button that opened the door.

"You should be able to reach a column from the hallway."

And so everyone walked out into the hallway. But as Sister Cecilia was about to leave, Professor Panda tapped her on the shoulder.

"What?" she asked the panda petulantly.

"Miss, I'd like to talk to you a moment."

"So talk."

"I've read of Geburah," said Professor Panda to Sister Cecilia, "I am very sorry for my faux pas. I thought at first, it was semantic but I realize…"

Sister Cecilia grew steely-eyed.

"Yes. It was the worst place imaginable. The Morality

Front's dogmas had completely deprived the world of pleasure. Most of us did not even get to see our own bodies, since the armor grows and stretches as those born in it age. Time Pimp cut me out with the orgone cane, rehabilitated me and helped me rehabilitate the others. He usually doesn't stick his neck out, but he said he had something against the Etharch. Something big. I don't blame him. The Etharch is one of the most rotten creatures ever born. I hope to never meet that monster. He ruined my life, ruined my planet."

"I know," said a very solemn panda, "and that's why I had to apologize. Nobody was from Anhedonia. Nothing grew or prospered there. It is horrible to claim that was someone's planet of origin."

"Thank you for understanding, Professor," she said, planting a kiss on the panda's cheek.

Time Pimp walked back into the room.

"So, everyone's calling for a hot tub orgy, bitch," he said, "and we're gonna need somebody to hand out the spankings."

"I do love hot tubs."

"Hmph," Time Pimp snorted, "The fuck do I care what ho's love?"

Sister Cecilia slid out of her habit, revealing the red synth-leather one piece bathing suit beneath it. While the habit made claims of Sister Cecilia's figure, the one piece substantiated them. Her small body was all legs and curves, though tight where it was absolutely necessary. She reached into the generous bodice of the suit pulling out a portable cat o' nine tails, playfully spanking Professor Panda with it.

"Oh my!" The panda giggled.

The hos had been waiting in the casino's giant Fank Toblerone-shaped hot tub as they had been instructed, practicing the arts of pleasure and pain on one another. Though Time Pimp was a good pimp, he was a stern one and he would not have permitted them to be out of the hot tub circulating among the high rollers where they could be lured away from Time Pimp's service or just distracted. Hos were very distractible and nobody had time for that nonsense. Shark girls, cowgirls, Viking girls, geisha girls, flapper girls, cavegirls, cybergirls, genetically modified leopard girls, and leather nuns were frolicking, cavorting, splashing, masturbating, penetrating, biting, splashing and playing. One at a time, the historical figures slid off their clothes and entered, and one at a time they found themselves amazed that the murder they had witnessed felt like it had occurred one-hundred years before. They were in the hands of Time Pimp's girls and Time Pimp's girls knew their stuff.

Mohandas Gandhi's delicate hunger-stricken body was capably manhandled by a Viking shieldmaiden, rubbing his bald head between her gigantic warrior breasts and wrapping hands that taught Christians a lesson around his manhood, rejuvenating it, rendering it the most vital part of his whole wearied body. A naked Sylvia Plath, slender but surprisingly toned for a New England patrician, swam up to him, nibbling his earlobe and massaging his testicles. She did so histrionically, making loud "ooh" noises so that Time Pimp knew she was enjoying herself.

"Only bitches get jealous," he thought to himself. As Sister Cecilia whipped Ayn Rand's arrogant objectivist ass and Sylvia played with the Mahatma's balls, Time Pimp was jealous like a bitch. The two geishas that had pulled down his red velvet speedo to massage his orgone manhood were not good enough.

Lord Byron had found a green-haired, heavily-pierced thirty-fifth century, full-body tattooed painslut to sodomize, with giant nipple rings to hang onto as he did. Being a painslut she was accustomed to being so roughly used and took a giddy thrill in the lack of lube in the situation.

"Ooh, yes," Byron moaned, "I'm the wickedest man there is!"

Time Pimp concentrated upon the hot tub around him, trying to remember the alchemical structure of a low-proof champagne. While pimps knew little of science, Time Pimp was damn good at alchemy, particularly at turning water into wine. Soon the champagne was soaking into everyone's skin or through their girls or through the anal exhaust pipes of the robot hos who, while perhaps a bit much for the fleshly clients, were content with pleasuring each other with specially modified pleasuredrills.

Sylvia, made brave and amorous by the champagne, dove down between the shieldmaiden's legs, filling her mouth with wine-drenched Viking wetness as from behind her, Lao Tzu held up by her legs and thrust into her. He was full of champagne and this was the right thing to do. Caligula bit down on the furred nipples of a cheetahgirl and full of boldness and sociopathic ego, slid three fingers into her feline pussy. She growled with discontent, clamping down her teeth on his shoulder. Though bone was clearly snapping under her great cat jaws, the Roman emperor was rather undeterred. Sherlock Holmes apathetically puffed his pipe as the sharp teeth of a wereshark whore worked his cock gently as they could. Two henna'ed eyebrow-ringed goth chicks took the initiative so they might worship their idol, Edgar Allan Poe, kissing him all over.

Time Pimp had hoped that bathing in champagne would not get to him and that it would not take his mind off the geishas but he was bathing in champagne and his judgment challenged and Sylvia bathing in champagne with judgment challenged and soon, they were disengaged from the amorous entanglements they'd once had and they were back in each other's arms and their lips once more pressed against each other's lips and bodies once more grinding. Soon Sylvia was bent against the wall of the hot tub and Time Pimp's glowing orgone was inside her. Time Pimp had been told to give up his orgone very seldom, to let his girls worship and kiss it but not to let it inside a woman. He had been surprised how much he liked it inside of Sylvia and that once again, in spite of himself and the tragedy and the fortress of male stoicism he had built, he was back there floating in alchemical champagne. History descended into a big ball of flesh around him and in her flesh he once more became one with his own history. Whether he liked it or not.

The orgy came to a sweaty, drunk, exhausted conclusion and everyone stepped out of the hot tub and dressed again. They were relieved, they were relaxed and they were once again involved in investigating a murder that had just recently occurred.

"Well, shit," said Time Pimp as though the hot tub orgy could have solved the murder but had just barely come up short of doing so. Everyone else seemed to be in agreement.

"My dear Time Pimp, your hos were sensational as always," said Sherlock Holmes, "but I fear we are still faced with the task of tracking down whatever archfiend committed these murders. And I don't think we'll be able to find the killer with another hot tub orgy."

"Wouldn't hurt to try," Byron chimed in.

"I concur," Ayn Rand purred, her hand on Caligula's crotch.

"We should split up and see if we can find anyone who saw anything suspicious or find evidence of where the killer found the weapons," Gandhi suggested.

"Agreed," said Time Pimp, "I'll go with Professor Panda."

He did not want Professor Panda's company, but the panda was the person in their company that he trusted least. He wanted to make sure he could keep his eyes on one of the tyrants of the 42$^{nd}$ Century. This was probably all the work of the panda. After all, the panda had access to some sort of time travel device so could have committed the murder in seconds, or frozen time with a Posthuman Timestream Stunning Device and done it with nobody the wiser. He had learned some things during his adventures with Sherlock Holmes.

They went together to Toblerone's private office, a Fank Toblerone-shaped chamber decorated with dozens of pictures of grilled cheese sandwiches, which made sense because Toblerone was a big wheel in the Grilled Cheese Consortium, possibly even the leader if one could hold dominion over grilled cheese. There was a half-eaten gingerbread house on Toblerone's desk, which Time Pimp tore a piece off of.

"I understand you," said Professor Panda, "we are not that different, you and I. We are first of all part of the grand fraternity of chrononauts."

"Chrononauts? I can't even hear jiveass words like that. Who the fuck says that?"

"Yes, I suppose pimps prefer more colloquial speech than pandas. This is true."

"Damn straight."

"But we have more in common than that," said Professor Panda as he scanned the instrument in his hand, "I don't know if you know…"

Time Pimp scowled.

"Yeah, I know and that's one of the reasons I don't like your fluffy black-and-white ass."

"Yes. Our race ruled the Earth. We waited until you thought we were at our weakest then we revealed our intellect and ability to procreate rapidly. And we did subjugate humans and subject them to radical pain experiments, then mutate the most resilient of them and leave them on a planet whose resources would dwindle quite rapidly. The majority of pandas are truly rotten bastards. Which is why I became obsessed with time travel. I wanted to go to other times, to gather the weapons and knowledge of how to stop my race from making all of those mistakes. I am rebelling against what it means to be a panda."

Time Pimp yawned.

"Your speech is awfully boring. I don't see what it has to do with me neither. So what if you're trying to act like you're better than being a panda? I've spent days on Earth during the Panda Conquest. Pandas are disgusting."

Professor Panda chuckled.

"You know what race we find disgusting? Yours. There's a saying: better to be a panda than to pander!"

Time Pimp turned his back on Professor Panda.

"You don't know what you're talkin' 'bout, Panda. We didn't conquer the Earth and enslave all the humans. We didn't send up early genetic experiments into space that would evolve into the lionheads. We ain't nowhere near as bad as any jiveass pandas!"

"You enslave everyone. You buy and sell intimacy, you keep wonder under control with money and violence. Pimps have subjugated virtually every race on the planet to satisfy the urges of other species. If you would call yourselves anything but tyrants, you are mistaken."

Time Pimp turned back around, raising his backhand threateningly.

"You don't know me! You don't know about pimpin'!"

"I know that you control the most powerful forces in the universe and you use them for nothing, other than to make money that nobody ever really sees you spending."

"This is a new hat!" Time Pimp shouted, before taking his leave of Professor Panda. He had never thought he would ever be lectured on morality, especially by a creature as loathsome as a panda, a species that played dumb and tugged human heartstrings for millennia just to let loose a master plan and put the Earth through some of the worst hell it had ever endured. Odd that a panda would care about such a thing. Odd that a panda had even bothered. Perhaps this panda was somehow better than other pandas, but he was still very annoying. Time Pimp slammed his hand into the first column he could, not knowing exactly what it was he was looking for.

When he found what he had been looking for, he was angry. He had sought to avoid her for so long and there she was at the bar with Rand.

"Find anything?"

"Miss Plath's clitoris," said Rand, licking her lips.

Time Pimp shook his head.

"Motherfuckers are dead, bitch. This is serious."

"So is Sylvia's pussy."

"I think," said Sylvia bashfully, "that maybe we should be finding the killer."

"The killer," said Time Pimp, "is Professor Panda. Mystery solved. That jiveass black and white turkey has been playing us like a cheap keytar from the beginning. And you know what? I'm gonna find him and beat his ass."

"I think," said Sister Cecilia, "that you might be jumping to conclusions."

"Ain't no other conclusion to jump to. Pandas are motherfuckin' trouble."

"Fine," said Sylvia, "why don't you ask the column to take you to Professor Panda?"

"Maybe I will."

"I'm going to find Caligula," said Rand, "I have no self control because I'm a disgusting sociopath."

"Yeah," said Time Pimp, "you go do that. There's a good chance you might get stabbed."

"Later, inferiors!" said Rand, teleporting off.

And so Sylvia, Time Pimp and Sister Cecilia teleported to Professor Panda. Who had retreated to his study to get something. The study, it turns out, was in quite a state.

Two white paws were rested on the panda's desk beside the clockwork time gizmos he had devoted himself to so completely. Two legs were laid out beside the chair on which rested the labcoated torso of the Professor. Sitting upon his bookshelf, deprived of goggles, black ringed eyes open all too wide with horror was the head of Professor Panda, who was very, very dead. Behind his shades, the pimp shed a tear for the dead panda. He had found Professor Panda's exuberance annoying, he had not approved of what he had to say about pimps. He had mostly disliked the fuzzy black-and-white son of a bitch, but the panda was innocent and he was trying to be better than his people. Time Pimp, who cared deeply for Sylvia and for Cecilia, had indeed been very unlike pimps as he knew them and the panda had been very unlike pandas as he knew them.

"Shiiit," said Time Pimp.

"We're going to die here," said Sylvia, head hanging, "and I don't mind very much. I have lived, I suppose, and I have only a husband, children, and an unloving life to go back to."

Time Pimp wrapped his arms around her and planted a light, tender, fatherly kiss upon her cheek.

"Don't you say nothin' like that! Don't you cry like a bitch! We're gonna find this killer and you're gonna get out of this alive. Nobody's gonna die!"

He shuddered at the thought of what had happened to Dante, and the grief he felt when she had first taken leave of him. Grief. Attachment. These feelings were for bitches. He wanted to do everything he could to escape from them.

"This is the end of time," said Sylvia, sobbing, "everyone here is gonna die."

***

Elsewhere, Mohandas Gandhi was being led blindfolded down a tunnel with a gun pressed against his back. He could hear a door shut behind him. He could hear wild applause. He could feel a pair of mechanical hands give him an object. A sword. This was unusual. He had never held a sword before and had more or less no reason to start. But before he could utter any protestation, a heavy blow fell on his head and he went down. As he lost consciousness, he heard more of this wild applause. Had he not been wearing his blindfold, Gandhi would have seen the roboroo and the arena and the hungry buzzards and the crowd cheering on his gladiatorial debut, accidental or otherwise. But he had been blindfolded. And he had been knocked out. And buzzards with scalpels in their beaks cut him open so they could feast on the organs of one of the worst gladiators the arena had ever known.

Caligula and Byron had paired up. This pair up was not specifically to find the killer. In fact, Caligula was hoping the killer had already found and murdered everyone to teach them a lesson in the inevitability of getting murdered. Which, when imparted by Caligula was a very real lesson.

Byron and Caligula had chosen the loudest, ugliest, most overstimulating section of casino floor. Giant Roulette wheels were everywhere, stopping when the long-nose, tapirlike creatures strapped to them barked for them to do so. Energy waiters handed trays of exotic grilled cheese sandwiches to the victors, who would either walk away or trade up for rarer, more exotic cheeses. Low-impact slot machines traded a kiss on a mouth-shaped instrument panel for a chance to win compliments. When the user lost, the mouth would shout out one of the user's embarrassing secrets.

"Ah, gambling," said Lord Byron, "the great pastime of history's finest rakes and scoundrels, of which I am the finest."

Lord Byron approached a slot machine, eager to try his luck. His luck, it turned out, was something that was not going to get him very far. The Emperor Caligula had been trailing Byron, not only because he felt he was surely the prime suspect but also because he was starting to grow tired of Byron's boasts of supreme wickedness. For a man who took as much pride in his wickedness as Caligula did, this was not just tiresome but downright insulting. And Caligula was not going to tolerate it at all.

He waited for Byron to put in the quarter and start to reach for the lever. It would not be sufficient to murder a man after he had his slot machine play. No, Caligula was wickeder than that. He had every intention of letting Byron think he was about to play the slots and then not just kill him but steal his slot play. Before Byron could reach for the lever, Caligula's gladius was in his back. The Romantic poet let out a gasp then hit the floor, only to be unceremoniously stepped on by the insane Caesar who pulled the lever on the slot machine.

Four symbols appeared on the screen. A leech. A leech. A leech. A leech. Caligula had played these slots at the beginning of his trip and he had never seen a leech symbol. Odd. The slot machine made a "You win" sound. And the coin slot began shooting out hundreds of leeches at Caligula, grafting themselves to the emperor's face and body, sucking out his blood and fluids. He flailed about trying to get them off himself but to no avail, it was a swarm of them and their suckers were strong. He could feel their tiny teeth and suckers expel the life from his body.

"I'm still alive," he said quite literally anemically, before he and the veracity of his statement hit the floor.

\*\*\*

Time Pimp placed his hand upon a teleportation column, thinking "Suspects..."Sister Cecilia did the same. Fast as the speed of thought the two were borne through spacetime across the casino and dropped off into a dingy, plain dungeon. There did not seem to be suspects gathered here. Instead of suspects, there was nothing but a plain brick wall and a lonely megachronolapse camera hanging overhead. The contrast with the bright lights and overstimulation more than evident, it was as if they had been brought to some sad minimalistic improv night at a Mafia warehouse.

"Looks like that column was flat-out busted," said Time Pimp, very disappointed.

"What if it wasn't?" asked Cecilia.

"Well," said Time Pimp, "Sherlock Holmes would say that when you eliminate the impossible, whatever remains, however improbable, must be the correct solution. And he is one smart motherfucker."

"That solution would be that somebody is behind that brick wall."

"Then I guess we gotta pull back those bricks."

Sure enough, when Time Pimp and Cecilia pulled back the bricks, they were greeted by a familiar face. A familiar dead face. The sick fuck that had recently made short work of Professor Panda had a sense of humor. They had walled up Edgar Allan Poe without food or oxygen. Lao Tzu and Holmes entered the room, with a very concerned Sylvia Plath immediately trailing them. Seeing the corpse, Sylvia emitted an ungodly scream.

"Poe! Poe! Poe!"

Lao Tzu took a big swig from his flask.

"Miss Plath might be ruled out as suspect."

"Indeed," said Holmes, puffing his pipe, "I don't take her for any kind of actress. So, this leaves Lao Tzu, the suspicious Madam Rand, Time Pimp and Sister Cecilia. So, I deduce that the killer is…"

"You," said Time Pimp, charging up the pain in his orgone cane, "you're the killer. I couldn't be sure without more evidence, like, say, everybody around us dropping dead, but I know Sherlock Holmes and you ain't Sherlock Holmes. Sherlock don't get off if Watson don't write it down. And he only gets with white girls because he's a stone-cold racist."

"Brilliant deduction, my dear Time Pimp," he said, casually drawing Holmes' revolver and shooting Lao Tzu in the face. "Yes, I murdered almost everyone. Before you came here, I stole the casino's schematics, rigged the slot machines to emit leeches when Caligula touched them and hid the weapons in Toblerone's sitting room. Poe has been in this room for a couple of hours but with some sleight of hand I implanted a metabolic accelerator in his drink during the hot tub orgy. A couple of hours behind a stone wall in the dungeon was therefore more than enough to dispatch him. You're surprisingly clever, Time Pimp. But you're also going to be quite dead."

Laughing, Sherlock Holmes pulled out his eyeballs, revealing them to be false. His actual eyes were pink, pupilless and judgmental. His face, unlike Time Pimp's, was pale, though the features were identical. The deerstalker hat disappeared and in its place there was a miter of hard latex. His body was enveloped by flowing rubbery robes and in his hand, he held a hard latex staff topped by a woman's head. It stank heavily of formaldehyde. He wore no shoes and his feet had no toes. At this moment, it occurred to Time Pimp just why Byron's club foot had always bothered him so much.

"Death Pimp!" Time Pimp shouted, calling out the name of his vengeful twin brother. He had hoped he would never have to use that name again. He had hoped time was big enough for the two brothers until Death Pimp could finally realize that death was a natural process, and that there was no resisting it and they would finally be able to go together to the absinthe sea. But this was not in the nature of Death Pimp.

"Grand Etharch Pope Death Pimp to you, brother! You are, as always, disrespectful. It is a shame our father and uncle raised me so much better."

Time Pimp scoffed at his brother's accusation. Each time they met, Death Pimp would say this and each time they met, Death Pimp always followed this up with something repugnant.

"HA! I'm the disrespectful one? I don't think I'm the one who pimps out dead people to pay for his jiveass space church!"

"WRONG!" screamed Death Pimp, "all beings are dead since they will eventually be dead. Especially here. Every one of these hos you've brought are already dead by now. All things are dead here except for pimps since pimps are eternal if they do not go to the sea."

If repugnance was the intent, Death Pimp certainly did not fail with his next trick. The corpse of Mohandas Karamchand Gandhi shambled down the hall, slowly, awkwardly, as if the return from death had brought it to a kind of infancy once again, which made some sense since it was after all a new life. Time Pimp and Sister Cecilia did not like the look of this at all. Sister Cecilia had heard of Death Pimp's activities before but had not imagined that she would witness the depravity of Time Pimp's evil brother. Sylvia clutched Time Pimp's right arm and Sister Cecilia his left. Both were hanging on very tightly.

The shambling Mahatma stood before the one who summoned him, looking up expectantly, which seemed strange since the dead had no reason to expect anything.

"Turn around," Death Pimp ordered Gandhi, and he did.

"No," said Time Pimp, shaking his head in disbelief, "you can't!"

Time Pimp reached for the orgone cane and Sister Cecilia for her cutlass, but both stopped abruptly when Sister Cecilia felt the very familiar nudge of a laser pistol at her back. Someone had gotten the drop on her and since there were only three suspects left alive and one of them was one of the worst people in the history of mankind, they knew full well which one it was.

"You vill vatch," said Ayn Rand from behind Sister Cecilia, "and you vill like it."

This was not good. Time Pimp had no idea how he was going to get out of this one and did not relish the only thing that could come next. Death Pimp was rubbing the bony naked back of the Mahatma, cooing and giggling to himself like a baby. His hands moved down, kneading Gandhi's barely there asscheeks and then squeezing them hard. The man famous for passive resistance could give no resistance of any kind, since he was dead. An oily magenta serpent of orgone sprang out from under Death Pimp's latex robe. It was making a humming sound as it expanded, its head brushing against Gandhi's anus, rubbing it and caressing it, its hums softly begging for it to open.

"He can't!" gasped Sylvia.

"Please, don't, you can't do this," Sister Cecilia pleaded.

"Sick son of a bitch!" shouted Time Pimp.

"It is sick to engage in intercourse with the living," said Death Pimp, whose energy cock was working its way into Gandhi's ass, "they have hopes and dreams and ideas. You mustn't rot them with your genitals, brother. You must wait until a bit of rot and decay sink in so you can use the body in its state of unflappable innocence. This body is so beautiful and so innocent. It's a shame you are too base and disgusting to enjoy it, dear brother."

"If anyone closes their eyes, I will shoot this little bitch," said Ayn Rand in top form.

Even in death, Gandhi's stick-figure legs were trembling from the force of Death Pimp's thrusts. Death Pimp stuck his hand into the massive hole in the back of the great man's bald, flailed head. His fingers squirmed through brains, sending shocks of sensory delight down to Death Pimp's hips, which were devoting all of their energy to thoroughly and viciously fucking Gandhi. Time Pimp breathed deep knowing he would get only one chance to do it right but he also knew that if he did not try it was more likely that Death Pimp would have Sister Cecilia shot so he could pimp her corpse to the Morality Front's unspeakably vile patrons.

With lightning reflexes, Time Pimp pointed the orgone cane at Ayn Rand, sending a shiver of pleasure through the Objectivist's firm, lovely, evil body. Since Rand's hold had relaxed on the pistol, Sister Cecilia was able to draw her cutlass, which she used with one swift motion to cut Ayn Rand's nicotine-ravaged throat. Rand fell to the floor dead. Sylvia turned to run. Death Pimp pulled out of Gandhi, who fell motionless to the ground just as Rand had. Furious, Death Pimp, malformed orgone still exposed, tapped the floor with his staff.

They came out of small, sanitized timewombs, dozens of them, dressed in their head-to-toe latex armor. They formed a circle around Time Pimp, Sylvia and Sister Cecilia. Death Pimp reached into his robe, pulling out a gun and casually taking aim at his brother. On the megachronolapse camera on the ceiling, Time Pimp took a bullet to the head, died then stood up. In Cecilia and Sylvia's eyes, Time Pimp took a bullet to the head and survived it, the wound sealing back up.

"Why do you even bother?" Time Pimp asked, "You have to kill me at every point in time to get rid of me."

Death Pimp responded by squeezing off five headshots.

"I know. And someday I will. For right now, I'll just have to be content killing you as many times as I possibly can. At least until I can perfect the Perpetual Annihilation and Impurification Device."

"You clearly haven't," said Sister Cecilia, "because he exists right now."

"I don't know how time travel works," said Death Pimp nonchalantly, killing his brother once more, "nor do I care."

Time Pimp squeezed his fist white. He let out a low growl.

"He's right. Pimps don't know nothin' about science. I wish I'd talked to that panda more."

Death Pimp erupted into a screaming laugh.

"Oh, he was delightful! He taught me nothing about time travel but I felt exquisite tearing up his tiny body. Have you ever heard pandas scream? For all their veneer of civilization, he was in the end a wounded animal. Everything is in the end a wounded animal. You'll all make noises like stupid, rough beasts when we're done with you and reanimate your corpses to pimp them. I wish I hadn't made such a mess, that panda would have been such a prime piece of ass. So many perverts out there would pay to have their way with—"

"SHUT UP!" Cecilia screamed. She struggled and pushed enough to gain a foot-and-a-half of ground. With a powerful mule kick, she buried her heel in the latexed crotch of the Morality Front goon behind her. She headbutted the one to her right in the chest, hoping to get them to give slightly.

"Futile," said Death Pimp, "my minions are brainwashed and covered in latex. You cannot inflict pain on them. And don't even think of trying to hit them with an orgone burst, brother. Yes, I think I'm probably just going to chain you to the bumper of that gaudy car of yours and drive you back and forth through the entirety of time, from here at the end to the beginning, effectively annihilating you at every moment of existence without having to build what is no doubt a very expensive Perpetual Annihilation Device."

Time Pimp thought back to the orgone burst Dante had helped him generate with the force of his ecstatic grief. The lionheads were also immune to pain, but he had managed to get the time stream itself to eradicate them by reversing the Perpetual Torment and Suffering Device. It was too bad he didn't have a Perpetual Torment and Suffering Device...

Or did he? Time Pimp's brain exploded to life with an idea.

"Cecilia, you're a dominatrix! You can get these guys! Sylvia, you're one of the most tragic, sad, and moving poets in the history of motherfuckin' literature, stone-cold sadness. Use your words!"

Sylvia spoke up about the freedom of riding on her horse, the perfected woman, the scarlet stripper. She talked about the ecstasies of pain, the suffering and joys she endured at the hands of the wrong man that she had fallen in love with, about suicide as liberation, about loss and madness and the schism of reality. She recited the lines fast and fierce, barely giving them time to get into the forebrains of the condom-armored Morality Front goons, who backed away from her, utterly uncertain of what to make of the new emotional information in their dogma-addled brains. One pointed his latexed finger at his head, letting loose a high-speed latex bullet that splattered his brains through his armor.

Meanwhile Sister Cecilia was wrestling herself free from the Morality Front cultists, applying a series of swift spanks and nerve strikes.

"Dirty dirty little pigs! Fucking sluts! You like it when I beat you, don't you? Makes your tiny little cocks hard, doesn't it! Stirs your dirty shameful parts!"

The Morality Front cultists she was hitting were letting out small sounds of joy. The ones beside them too had erections pushing against and moisture growing in their latexed shells. Some of them had gotten the idea to spank each other, to choke themselves autoerotically or hold their breath for a long time. The one behind Time Pimp was cooing as she humped his leg. Sylvia's recitation was bringing some of them to suicide, forcing others to let loose tears and getting others to look to their brethren for catharsis, indulging in oddly gleeful sadomasochism.

"What are you doing? Death Pimp screamed at them, "I told you to dispose of them! Annihilate!"

The Morality Front cultists breathed heavier, stroked and spanked and molested harder. Death Pimp's disapproval and Cecilia's sexy reprimand and Sylvia's dark but life-affirming poetry were becoming the same thing to them. Death Pimp stopped shooting Time Pimp and began shooting some of his own men, with about the same efficacy. The bullets had a very difficult time penetrating the latex suits, though every clip or so, he managed to a blast hole into one of his minions and bring it down.

Time Pimp, unhanded by Morality Front cultists, advanced on his brother, giving him a pimp fu kick to the face with his platform shoe. He followed up with a blast of orgone from the cane, his famous backhand and a hard smack on the head. Death Pimp reeled from Time Pimp's superior pimpish fighting style, unable to get in any hits with wild swings from his staff. Time Pimp was not sure what he could do the invincible Death Pimp, but until he could figure it out, his nefarious brother was in for a world of pain. Although, so too was Time Pimp.

A Morality Front cultist, confused and overzealous grabbed hold of Sylvia, who bravely continued her recitation. The woman is perfected. The words dropped like an atomic bomb as the Morality Front goon's finger converted into a latex pistol pointed at his head, which he nudged against Sylvia's. The projectile flew through the side of the cultist's head, exiting out Sylvia's. In chunks of blood and skull fragment, the thing that had distanced Time Pimp from Sylvia and Sylvia from Time Pimp, the thieving death called suicide deprived Time Pimp of the woman he once loved, as a woman, as a friend, as a ho. Time Pimp was dazed, eyes glued to the spectacle of Sylvia's demise and that was just enough time for Death Pimp to make his move.

Powered by black orgone, Death Pimp pointed his staff at the broken body of Sylvia Plath who stood up, face stained with brains eyes dead and distant. "You failed me again. You failed me again. You can't keep your hos in line. You can't keep your life in line. You failed. You'll always fail."

"You ain't alive!" the traumatized pimp screamed. "You ain't alive!"

The reanimated Plath stumbled toward Sister Cecilia, who had barely had time to register that Sylvia had even been killed. Even the resolve of the leather nun was not enough for her to swing her sword at the reanimated poetess. Cecilia threw down her weapon, letting Sylvia get two hands around her throat.

"Take me to the Cadillac and let me do my business with you and maybe I won't make her part of my stable of dead hos. You are weak, brother. You can't keep your women and your life in line. You're no good to any of these people. You're the one who wants to go to Netzach someday and go to the absinthe to change."

Death Pimp pointed the staff again and a reanimated Rand stood up to nod in agreement.

"Yes, an inferior specimen. No good to anyone."

Though Sylvia was dead and Cecilia was threatened, Time Pimp gave no indication that he accepted Death Pimp's offer. He thought about what Lao Tzu had said about Toblerone murdering himself. Toblerone's murderer had come to him. Plath's murderer would always come to her. Death Pimp had thought to escape death forever, which should have been easy enough for an immortal but it wouldn't be. He would one day have to join Time Pimp becoming octopi in someone's shoes or his murderer would come. Or both. He remained dead silent. If he sacrificed himself, it wouldn't be like the man he'd been jealous of, there would be no meaning.

The door burst open and a bunch of gingham-clad old ladies rushed in.

"Grand Etharch Death Pimp," declared their leader, "you are wanted by the Wealthy Dowager's Supper Club!"

A dozen more old ladies flooded in, then a dozen more, each of them eagerly brandishing a fork and a knife. The Morality Front, thoroughly confused by all of the sexuality and suicide, sadism and masochism were too busy beating, murdering and fondling themselves and each other to do anything as the old ladies rushed in, making their way toward Death Pimp. Death Pimp's attention focused completely on the old ladies, zombie Plath relaxed her grip on Sister Cecilia's neck, allowing the leather nun to break free.

The supper club wrestled Death Pimp to the floor, shoving their forks and knives into him, pulling off bits of flesh and eating them, until he was stripped to bones and organs, which with both great precision and animal hunger, they pulled from him and ate. Death Pimp being immortal, these organs quickly replaced themselves, as did his flesh. The Wealthy Dowager's Supper Club had found the most exciting and perfect meal they could imagine and they would be sated by it literally until the end of time.

Sister Cecilia and Time Pimp fled until they could find a teleportation column, which took them back to the hot tub in which the hos were waiting. Gathering them together, the two made their way out to the Purple Cadillac which Time Pimp anxiously started, calling forth the timewomb. As they drove through the pink tunnel, Time Pimp was silent, grateful for the sweet, feminine timedew condensing on his face as he drove toward Netzach. He was crying. Like a bitch.

He had once taken Sylvia back to her husband and children, knowing her fate and how he most likely could not undo it. Or could he? He did not know how time travel worked, but thinking of Sylvia was one of the few times he cared. Fuck bitches. Get paid. That should have been it. But it was not. He missed her and he had lost her again. And he had lost her again to the brother he could never stop, the brother that would hate him forever.

But Time Pimp, being a pimp and unaware of time travel did not understand the nature of the end of time. The end of time was the last thing that would happen and the casino itself was suspended at the end of time. There was but one casualty in the murders at the Time Casino and that was Fank Toblerone, who, as Lao Tzu had forewarned, had brought on his own murderer by gathering the suspects together. Poe still wandered the streets of Baltimore, rabid-screaming gibberish in his last day. Lao Tzu still died in peace on a mountaintop somewhere. Ayn Rand still succumbed to cancer. Professor Panda still bounded through the time stream. Caligula was still killed by his own soldiers. Jesse James still betrayed by his own gang. Lord Byron still dead in a yacht. Gandhi still assassinated and Sylvia, his beloved Sylvia, still died with her head in an oven as he always knew she had. Time Pimp's one consolation after the whole ordeal was that Death Pimp was gone, eaten forever by the ravenous Dowager's Supper Club. But this, like all Time Pimp knew of time travel, was wrong.

# THE VIENNA JOB

# JOB

## 1911

The Vienna Job had gotten wildly out of hand. Sister Cecilia was slapping Teddy Roosevelt awake as he sat in his Oval Office chair gazing onward into space and stewing in a puddle of his own cum. Time Pimp was at Mexican standoff with Ka'ssen the Blue Beast whose throbbing forehead vagina had entranced the president and was currently keeping his bear in line so that she could ride on his back. Time Pimp was about to let out an orgone burst from his cane, which might have caused Ka'ssen a certain amount of anguish but would have done little to the badger she had pointed in his direction, a badger that would surely fly off and pounce on him, causing him a great deal of pain and trouble and making good the escape that he could not let Ka'ssen the Blue Beast make good again.

## 7678, *The Planet Yod*

"Look, buddy," said the glittercloud, "you're better off leaving this alone."

Time Pimp let loose his backhand on the glittercloud, who in spite of being a cloud, let loose some dewy, glittery blood. Sister Cecilia did not know how Time Pimp hit a cloud hard enough to make it bleed, but decided it best not to think about such things. What was important was the cloud was hurt.

"Kjennen Ka'ssen. I need Kjennen Ka'ssen. She worked for my father."

"Yes. Only one pimp could have taught the pimphand like that. And only one pimp could have kept Ka'ssen the Blue Beast in line. It is an honor to meet the son of Julius Baker."

"Kjennen Ka'ssen."

The glittercloud tried to float off in the opposite direction, but Time Pimp was quick on the draw with the orgone cane. He had set it to pleasure, striking the cloud with an orgone burst that caused it to emit a series of electric snowflakes.

"Oh, no, you mustn't…"

The cloud got slightly smaller, it's voice higher as it protested. Time Pimp released another orgone burst. The cloud puffed up in size, made a farting noise and a pleasurable squeal. It let loose another round of snowflakes and after doing so, it shrank yet again.

"Okay. I'll cooperate. But you'll be sorry. Kjennen Ka'ssen is the trickiest ho in any time stream and there's a rumor she gets around with panda tech. Kjennen Ka'ssen is working for Squelatinous Quub, the hip hop mogul mostly composed of half-digested body parts from his enemies. You don't wanna mess with him."

"Don't got any choice," said Time Pimp, "there's no other way I can carry out the Vienna Job."

The glittercloud laughed, raining down drip drops of a pink lemonade-like substance.

"The Vienna Job?"

*5099, The Planet Netzach, Time Pimp's lounge*

Time Pimp was not quite drunk enough and he knew this. Sister Cecilia was not quite drunk enough and she knew this. And so more water became cognac. And more sobriety became fuzz and static. They melted slouched down, no longer sitting on but propped up by the beanbag chairs.

"I've been thinking," said Time Pimp, "about how failure is for bitches."

"Yeah," said Sister Cecilia, killing her cognac in one swallow, "bitches and hos."

"I am a pimp."

"And I am a trained and fully licensed leather nun."

"I gotta do somethin' big."

"Yeah," said Sister Cecilia pounding the table, "we gotta do something big. I got Genghis Khan's horse."

"Damn right, bitch!"

"And you got a Purple Cadillac that travels through time."

"Damn right, bitch!"

"You know what you should do?"

Time Pimp pounded the table.

"The Vienna Job!"

"The Vienna Job!"

*6400*

The Gangstabot librarians came forth, scimitar penises spinning, sideways gat hands aimed at Time Pimp and Sister Cecilia. It was a posse of about ten and they were not going down without a fight.

"Yo, mothafucka, we don't allow pimps in the library! Why don't you go fuck a duck!"

Time Pimp did not like Gangstabots. While some of the more sophisticated models were fond of hos out of habit, they lacked a fundamental ability to generate, utilize or be impeded by orgone and this was a big problem, especially when he needed access to something or someone they protected. He had to get ready to pimp fu them instead. Sister Cecilia drew her cutlass and decided that rather than risk getting shot, she'd have to charge.

The Gangstabots, being librarians, were not particularly good shots and were holding their gunhands sideways solely because it looked cool which made their aim even further off. It didn't take the quick and graceful sister long to close on them. She skillfully parried two scimitar cocks at once, disliking the idea of being penetrated by force as much as the idea of being cut.

With a spinning pimp fu hurricane kick, Time Pimp launched into the fray sending a doo-ragged Gangstabot head flying off as Sister Cecilia ducked and cut low, slicing a Gangstabot's golden pegleg off. The soft gold and the poorly attached heads were the main structural weaknesses of Gangstabots, particularly in the less combative models that acted as librarians. The one-legged Gangstabot stumbled to the floor, where Sister Cecilia got a chance to boot it in the face and then snap its flimsy neck with her thick heel. Before the other scimitar cock she'd been fending off could catch her in the arm, she rose up with a skillful parry, as Time Pimp came in with his pimp hand technique, which smacked the Gangstabot's head clean off.

The two remaining Gangstabots tried to shoot point blank, but still their aim was askew and it wasn't long before pimp hand and cutlass had managed to decapitate the both of them. The five Gangstabots had proven a less than formidable challenge though Time Pimp knew things were going to get worse for him since he had tangled with Squelatinous Quub. They would have to find Kjennen Ka'ssen quickly before the dead Gangstabots would start emitting distress calls.

They were lucky, or rather as lucky as anyone who had found the Blue Beast could be. Kjennen Ka'ssen, teal-skinned, hourglass, dressed in transparent synthsilk, was seated at a table in the psychology section and reading. The vaginal lips in her forehead were quivering. Time Pimp and Cecilia alike were very tempted to stick a finger in there, but did not since this would be beyond impolite.

"I was wondering," said Kjennen Ka'ssen, "how long it would take for you to track me down. It is a pleasure to meet you. You have your father's sense of style. Would you like to penetrate my brain? Cause I would like for you to fuck it."

"Not right now, Miss Ka'ssen. But it is a beautiful mind and the legends are true, you are a ho fo sho."

"Believe it, Pimp Daddy. I was good enough for your daddy and I am good enough to be one of yours."

Time Pimp was surprised.

"You mean you don't want to keep working for Squelatinous Quub?"

Kjennen Ka'ssen shook her head. A thin antlike feeler emerged from her shoulder to rub the outer lips of her forehead vagina.

"I'm afraid that I don't. See, Quub got mad at me and to punish me, sent me to this library. He demands several book reports a day or Mecha Charles Dickens Times Two gets called in."

Time Pimp shuddered. He had heard of Library Commissioner Mecha Charles Dickens Times Two and he did not much like the thought of coming up against him any more than he liked the thought of offending Squelatinous Quub. But he would have to do it, otherwise he would not be able to carry out the Vienna Job or to accumulate the reward for it, which was, naturally, quite substantial. He converted a nearby water fountain into a cognac fountain and filled his flask.

"Well," said Sister Cecilia, "we've killed the Gangstabots and are willing to offer you protection against Quub and the Library Commissioner."

"Bitch!" cried Time Pimp, "Don't do my business for me!"

Sister Cecilia hrumphed.

"Fine. Do you have anything to add?"

Time Pimp could think of nothing more to say. He emptied his flask to look like he was too important to answer her question.

Ka'ssen lit up.

"Really? You're saying you can offer me protection against Squelatinous Quub and the Library Commissioner if I do your job for you? Whatever it is, I'll take it," she said, "I want out of here. I'm tired of doing all of these book reports and I'm worried that eventually the Library Commissioner will show up. I'll take any job you offer, Pimp Daddy."

The feeler slid all the way into her forehead vagina. Her midnight-blue nipples hardened.

"Why, I'm so hard up, Pimp Daddy," she laughed, "that I'd even do the Vienna Job. So, if you're a real Pimp Daddy and you ain't a couple of lames, get me to the exit and your time travel device and Ka'ssen the Blue Beast is all yours."

"Glad to hear you say that," said Time Pimp, "cause we're gonna do the Vienna Job."

*4444, Earth*

Kjennen Ka'ssen was quite fetching in her knee socks, tight sweater, and leather miniskirt. She chewed her pen as she took notes, staring lasciviously at the lecturer, who was starting to have some trouble paying attention. The class was full of pandas, the lecturer was himself a panda and, for some reason, a sexy blue schoolgirl was taking notes in a twentieth-century spiralbound notebook and making nasty glances in his direction. Professor Panda enjoyed the luscious humanesque shape of her body. He had been fond of the human slaves in his father's harem and, though he loathed the way his people treated humans, he loved the feel of their hairless skin and their thin bony bodies. He cleared his throat and pulled up his goggles.

"Is there something you don't understand about the lecture, Miss…"

"Ka'ssen, Kjennen Ka'ssen."

Professor gulped loudly. He fidgeted with his tie.

"I am flattered by your presence, Miss Ka'ssen. The reputation of the Blue Beast precedes you."

Ka'ssen giggled girlishly.

"And yours as well, Professor Panda. You're well-known for your innovations in time travel theory. Perhaps we could chat after class?"

Professor Panda pulled a laser rifle out of his desk, pointing it at the class.

"Class dismissed!" he barked and the room cleared save for him and Ka'ssen the Blue Beast.

She got up on all fours on Professor Panda's desk.

"I have been dirty in class," she declared, "so very disruptive, Professor. I'm a very bad girl and you're a very bad panda."

Professor Panda picked up a yardstick near the holochalkboard, eagerly bringing it down on her blue ass. Her forehead vagina let out a short queef of laughter, which for reasons the panda did not understand made him very excited. He spanked her again, harder, and as he did grazed her perineum with a fuzzy finger. The forehead vagina queefed again and she let out a short "ooh." Another spanking followed and he gently inserted his finger into her anus, cautious of his claws. He liked the muscles contracting around him.

"Don't worry," she said, feeling his trepidation, "you can put out your claw. I often like to bleed inside a little."

"Oh, Miss Ka'ssen," said the panda, quickly swiping her insides with his nail, "you are such a dirty beast."

He spanked three more times, her ass bruising a lush forest-green, the color no doubt of the blood inside that was now on his claw. Her feelers emerged to finger herself, tickling her synapses and her vaginal walls alike, sending a rush through her body that made her respond with almost unsettling force to Professor Panda's fingering, fucking his little panda hand.

"Oh, Professor!"

"Oh, Miss Ka'ssen!"

She looked over her shoulder, a smile on her indigo lips.

"What do you think, Professor? Wanna fuck with my head?"

Any man would have.

*1920, Vienna*

The coketrain was shaking in the library commissioner's giant fist. They had gathered the sack of cocaine they needed but Mecha Charles Dickens Times Two had nonetheless gotten the drop on them and was ready to not just crush them but also to keep going and stomp the city as well. It was likely that everyone on the train would be crushed and everyone in Vienna as well, all because Time Pimp had chosen to undertake the most ill-advised Client in pimp history.

He hanged his head low.

"Well, looks like I'm gonna have to stick my neck out for two hos."

Kjennen Ka'ssen placed a hand on Time Pimp's shoulder. It felt good for a hand on his shoulder. It stirred his feelings and heart and orgone. Such was the touch of Ka'ssen the Blue Beast, supposedly the greatest ho in the history of all hos.

"Are you sure? If you stick your neck out for hos too much, then the Intergalactic Pimp Council…"

Time Pimp backhanded Ka'ssen dropping her to the floor of the train.

"Bitch! I don't care what those motherfucking turkeys gotta say, I gotta do what I think is right. Even if I don't know what that is."

Sister Cecilia clapped, eyes lighting up.

"Wait, doesn't Mecha Charles Dickens Times Two run on steam?"

"Bitch! Pimps don't know about science!"

Sister Cecilia was surprisingly patient.

"Well, he does. There's smoke coming out of his ears. And if he runs on steam, that means there needs to be water tanks in his head."

Time Pimp nodded.

"I get it."

"Good."

"Just cause we're gonna die, you think I'm gonna take you into the water tank and give you the cock. Well it didn't work in a real hot tub and it's not going to work now. I ain't never givin' a ho my cock!"

Ka'ssen stood up.

"No, sweetheart. That's not what she's saying at all. She's saying that if there's a water tank, you can turn it into wine or cognac with pimpish party alchemy and get him drunk, possibly destroying his brain or something."

Time Pimp thought about the idea for a second and tried to see if he could surpass it. He could not. All his other ideas involved either sex or violence, neither of which would be any good against Mecha Charles Dickens Times Two.

"I'm gonna miss you hos," he said before running out the door to get onto the library commissioner's giant metallic arm. The arm being gigantic and the library commissioner being nothing but a two-headed bronze statue of Charles Dickens running on steam power, Time Pimp was able to get on it unnoticed and, having the robust physique of a pimp, ran quickly up the library commissioner's shoulder and into his ear.

Sure enough, the library commissioner's brain was gears, pumps and pistons, all running on steam generated by a giant central water tank. Time Pimp concentrated on cognac, tempting the atoms to copulate with the water and make sweet alchemical love. He was exhausted, dizzy and weak by the end of it, overwhelmed by the glut of atoms he'd had to alchemically transmogrify. As the library commissioner began to wobble, so too did Time Pimp, whose vision was starting to go blurry from all the alchemical pimping.

He was about ready to faint, but found his fainting

stopped by a blue hand holding him up. Ka'ssen the Blue Beast brought Time Pimp to his feet, leading him out Mecha Charles Dickens Times Two's ear and back out onto his arm where Sister Cecilia was waiting. She was holding a big sack of cocaine.

*1978, Netzach*

"I don't like to disco," said Death Pimp, "it's stupid and the music is repetitive! I hate it!"

"Ha," said Julius Baker, father of Time Pimp and Death Pimp, "just like your uncle. Haters gotta hate."

"I'm ready!" Little Time Pimp was pointing emphatically in the air, a clumsy variation on the moves of John Travolta.

Kjennen Ka'ssen entered the lounge in a flowing white dress, which contrasted with her skin tone but brought out her body. The two young pimps let out a sigh. Though they grew up among hos, Kjennen Ka'ssen still took their breaths away and did the same for Julius Baker. She knelt down, smiling at Time Pimp.

"My! What moves you have, little Time Pimp! You'll be as good as your daddy in no time!"

Julius Baker laughed boisterously.

"Bitch, you best not delude the boy. Ain't no pimp ever gonna get moves smoother than Julius Baker, grand pimp daddy of them all!"

The very spitting image of Julius Baker entered, save that he was ghastly pale, dressed in all black and wearing no shades over his beady pink eyes. He had a switchblade in his black gloved hand.

"Your moves are 'bout as smooth as sandpaper, playa!"

Julius put up his fists.

"You'd best check yourself before you wreck yourself!"

"Haters must hate, you know the rules. I must be an example to little Death Pimp, so I have come here to cut up your finest ho."

"I ain't gonna let you do that, lame!"

Julius Baker and his Hater tussled. For a pimp fight, it was low-tech and not very graceful. Death Pimp rolled his eyes. He appreciated his father's affection for them, but did not like pimpin' drills like this. There was something inorganic about the struggles between this Playa and this Hater. The hate just didn't seem to be there. Then again, how much could Julius really hate his brother? At the time, Death Pimp did not hate Time Pimp much at all, so had trouble relating to the very arbitrary roles of Playa and Hater.

The Blue Beast patted little Death Pimp's head.

"I'm very proud of you. One day you're gonna hate a lot, Death Pimp. Poor Time Pimp's gonna have a very hard time thanks to you!"

Time Pimp let out a huff of contempt.

"Bitch, please! Who cares what a ho is proud of? Hos don't got no pride!"

Julius Baker, filled with rage, pimp handed his brother in the face and sent him flying, then stomped over to his son, very disappointed.

"I raised you better than that. Hos got respect when their pimp's got respect. You disrespect Ka'ssen, you disrespect me. You disrespect me, you disrespect yourself!"

"Yes," said Baker's brother, for some reason trying to choke back a sob, "your father is right, even though he's got no game and he smells bad. It is wrong to disrespect this ho. She is a fine-ass bitch though I wouldn't fuck her with your father's tiny dick."

The Hater was trying to muster sincerity and teach the boys, but the dictum that he had to hate was getting in the way. Ka'ssen smiled again, approached the Hater and kissed him on the cheek.

"Thank you," said Kjennen Ka's,sen, "I appreciate that."

She kissed both of the boys and knelt in front of Julius, exposing his orgone and tenderly fellating it. The Hater nearby heaved a blissful sigh which was confusing to the young pimps as any of this was, but showed perhaps that the life of a pimp, Playa or Hater was a complicated one and not as clearcut as they thought. Perhaps as well as hate, there was a trace of love in their Hater uncle's heart. Death Pimp thought perhaps that maybe he could try to love. He loved his father and he sort of loved Time Pimp, he supposed and he loved his uncle, so maybe he was not just obligated to hate.

Julius tried to maintain composure as Ka'ssen was massaging his orgone with her skillful mouth, but the Blue Beast was too much for him, causing him to ooh and aah and grunt and moan with joy and satisfaction. He clenched his fists to pallor to try to maintain focus during the superlative blowjob so that he could address his sons.

"You see, boys, this shit's important. You should never ever give up the cock for hos. If you give up the cock, you lose respect and she'll think you're some kind of bitch and we ain't bitches, we're pimps."

"If you don't give up the cock, then how are pimps born?" asked Death Pimp.

"Pimps ain't born," said Julius, "they're made."

"Made with cocks," said the Hater, rolling his pink eyes.

"Do you have to do that?"

"Yes. I gotta hate. I would think by now that would be more than abundantly clear."

Ka'ssen suddenly gagged and jerked. She released Julius' cock from her mouth. She turned around to find that she had just been hit by an orgone burst and to see both the cane that it came from and the pimp that wielded the cane. A glowering Time Pimp and an angry Sister Cecilia were standing in the doorway.

"Come with us and get into the goddamn car, bitch!" ordered Time Pimp.

The Hater snickered, but Julius Baker was furious.

"Bitches! You do not interrupt me when my fucking ho is pleasing and I am teaching my…"

Julius put his hand on his forehead.

"Fuck. You are a fucking idiot. I don't know how time travel works and I don't fucking care but I know that this shit's gotta be wrong."

"What's going on, daddy?" asked little Time Pimp.

"I think that's you," little Death Pimp explained, "and I think that you're a fucking idiot. This is most likely why I hate you."

Kjennen Ka'ssen vanished in a burst of light, leaving Time Pimp in the lounge looking foolish to his father, his uncle, his past self and to a young Death Pimp. This did not feel like one of the finer moments of his life. The Vienna Job had gotten wildly out of hand and there would be consequences. Since Time Pimp did not know or care how time travel worked, he did not know what these consequences would be. Though he did know one of these would be experiencing his father's famed backhand.

Which he did. Julius Baker launched his son across the room in one blow.

"Looks like you tried the Vienna Job and you failed. What did I always tell you? Huh?"

A dizzy Time Pimp tried to rise to his feet.

"I don't know. My head hurts."

"He said never try The Vienna Job," said young Death Pimp.

"That's right," said Time Pimp's uncle, "neither of you should ever try The Vienna Job. It will just get wildly out of hand."

"Wow," said Sister Cecilia, "your relationship with Kjennen Ka'ssen is really fucked up."

*1920, Vienna*

"I can only theorize," said Sigmund Freud, chomping on his cigar, "that you are a delusion brought on by stress."

Time Pimp, Cecilia and Ka'ssen folded their hands and waited for Freud to accept what was in front of him. He reached into a snuffbox in his jacket pocket and opened it. His face grew pale, his skin clammy. He started to sweat. He replaced the snuffbox and examined once more the three unusual personages on his couch, the voluptuous leather-clad nun, the strange overly tanned man dressed in red velvet whose shoes were filled with tiny octopi, and the teal-skinned vixen whose vagina was in the center of her forehead.

"I'm out of cocaine," he declared matter-of-factly, "this is very upsetting."

"I'm here to help you, Doctor Freud," said Time Pimp, "I'm here to give you what you want so we can build a better future."

"You don't look like a man who can publish my books or share my theories with others."

"Well," said Sister Cecilia, "we can help you with something else, something you're missing in your life."

"I'm the happiest man in the world," said Freud, making eye contact with nobody, "you people are free to leave. Especially since you are only delusions of my overworked imagination."

"So you're saying," said Ka'ssen, "that there is nothing that you want? That there has never been anything you've secretly longed for that you were afraid to share?"

"No."

"You're a lying bitch," said Time Pimp, "you're in denial."

"Hmm," said Freud, "denial. I like that. Let me write that down."

Freud jotted down the word in his notebook. He once again reached into his pocket for his snuffbox. Opened it. Found nothing. Returned it to his pocket.

"I'm out of cocaine," he repeated.

"This ain't about cocaine!" Time Pimp snapped.

"Can you get me some cocaine?"

"Yes," said Sister Cecilia, "all the cocaine you could want."

"Good," said Freud, still fidgeting with the snuffbox, "since I want a great deal of cocaine. I should have figured you were all involved in the drug trade."

"We aren't," said Time Pimp, getting slightly irate, "I don't deal in drugs. I'm a pimp."

"Not interested," said Freud.

"We can help you get with any woman you want. ANY woman."

Freud grew nervous.

"Who are you? Where are you from? How do you know? Does anyone else know? Nobody else can know!"

"Relax, Client," said Time Pimp, "we're not here to judge.

We're here to help."

"I want your help," he said, "but I can't…"

"You can't get it up without your cocaine?" Sister Cecilia finished.

"Yes, but there's a problem."

"Of course there's a problem," Time Pimp mumbled to himself, "always a fuckin' problem, isn't there?"

"I owe a great deal of money to my dealer so I will need somebody to steal a large sack of cocaine off of the incoming coke train."

Nobody bothered to ask why Freud needed an entire sack of cocaine or why it could not simply be attained right from the dealer by an intermediary. This was The Vienna Job. It was complicated.

*1870, Texas, The Black Saloon*

"Stay away from my woman, she ain't your whore no more!" the glowing blackhatted cowboy bellowed, voice joined by a chorus of ghosts. The decapitated gang of headless black-hatted bluejeanned, bespurred outlaws rose from the floor, pulling back the hammer on their Smith & Wessons at the same time.

Kjennen Ka'ssen buried her face in the cowboy's shoulder.

"Tell me when it's over, lover!"

"Don't you worry, Miss Ka'ssen. I'll get this pesky pimp out of the way, or I ain't the Tartarus Kid!"

Time Pimp threw down his cane and threw up his hands. Sister Cecilia followed his lead and threw her cutlass to the floor.

"Listen up," said Time Pimp, "you been had, man. This woman's the most dangerous whore in the world. She gone and absconded with googleplex spacebucks implanted in her DNA!"

The glowing cowboy wizard made a face.

"I don't know what any of those words, mean, sir."

"It means, cowboy, that you done been had, too! She's only on the run from me because she stole more than you can imagine."

"This true, darling?" asked the Tartarus Kid.

"Are you going to believe a pimp?" Ka'ssen asked, "Or are you going to believe me?"

She placed her hand on his crotch, making it clear that there was only one person in the room who was to be believed.

"Your story don't check out, Mister Pimp." The Tartarus Kid tossed Time Pimp and Sister Cecilia two gold coins apiece.

"Pay the ferryman when you get there."

"You're makin' a mistake, fool," said Time Pimp, "I bet she don't even suck your dick."

A puzzled Ka'ssen glared at Time Pimp.

"I suck his dick plenty."

"Not like you sucked mine or my daddy's."

The Tartarus Kid pulled his gun quickly, pointing at her.

"You fellated this man and his father?"

"Darling," cooed Ka'ssen, "that was different. My whoring days are over."

"Ha! She's still my ho."

The headless bandits turned toward their leader, wondering if they were supposed to fire their guns yet. The Tartarus Kid gave no confirmation.

"She ain't."

Time Pimp folded his arms.

"Well if she ain't, then she won't mind suckin' your dick right here."

"I'm sure she won't!" shouted back the Tartarus Kid.

"What are you doing?" Sister Cecilia whispered, "You're not gonna make me suck your dick, are you? I don't do that."

"Prove it!" Time Pimp shouted, ignoring Sister Cecilia altogether.

"He's trying to stall," Ka'ssen argued.

The Tartarus Kid's glow got dimmer.

"He's right. You won't do it."

"She won't," said Time Pimp, "you don't know how to keep your bitch in line."

"Suck me," said the Tartarus Kid to Ka'ssen.

"It's a trick!"

"Suck me."

Ka'ssen got on her knees, unbuttoning the Tartarus Kid and taking him into her mouth. She began to suck.

"You see?" said the Tartarus Kid, "She's my woman now."

Sister Cecilia caught onto Time Pimp's plan.

"Mmm, you're right. It takes a really powerful man to get a hot piece of ass like Ka'ssen to suck his dick in public."

The Tartarus Kid put away his gun, placing a hand on Ka'ssen's head in encouragement, sticking his pinky into the pussy on her forehead.

"Yes," he said, his voice growing slightly distant and trailing off a bit, "I am a very powerful man."

The headless bandits relaxed the grips on their guns, then dropped them. They wobbled, experiencing trouble standing. The gang of dead outlaws could feel their master's dominion over the situation starting to wane along with his concentration. Kjennen Ka'ssen, cock in mouth, finger in her brain, saw none of this, nor did the Tartarus Kid, who was closing his eyes to experience the oral delights of the finest whore who ever lived.

"That's right," said Time Pimp, "ain't nothin' like a ho chokin' down your dick in public to prove you're in control."

"Yes," mumbled the Tartarus Kid, "this is my woman."

The reanimated gang tumbled to the floor. Time Pimp, quietly as a man on giant platform shoes could, took a couple steps forward to grab one of their guns. Behind his shades, he did not so much as blink before squeezing off a shot and putting a bullet into the Tartarus Kid's heart. The Tartarus Kid opened his eyes, bleeding, dying and cumming in Kjennen Ka'ssen's mouth all at the very same time, and hit the floor, just as his gang had.

"Dark orgone," Time Pimp explained, "the wizards of The Black Saloon ain't wizards at all. This place was a front built by Death Pimp. Funny thing is, it's hard to maintain dark orgone when regular orgone's building up. Nobody ever controlled a horde of zombies while some bitch choked down their dick. It's every Hater's dream, but it ain't never gonna happen."

Ka'ssen the Blue Beast was quicker on the draw with her

Personal Time Sojourning Device than Time Pimp was with the revolver, though. Luckily, they had the radar device they'd gotten from Professor Panda. 1911. What could she have been doing there?

*3636, Yesod*

Young Time Pimp and Death Pimp were at a hovering table with their father and a camelheaded creature dressed in a top-of-the-line grilled cheese sandwich suit. Just below them in an icy sumo ring, Ken Shifatsu, Grand Sumo of Yesod was battling Byej Dogbane, a gorilla-sized flea who was giving him a run for his money. As the icy sumo ring was suspended over an active volcano, the event had an additional element of danger. It would have utterly transfixed Julius Baker and sons if it were not for the object the camelheaded beast had just set down on the table. It was a shining syringe full of flickering numbers.

"Do you know what this is?" the camel asked.

"I got a notion," said Julius Baker, turning his water into cookie dough and gulping it down.

"Genetic datastream," said young Death Pimp, "it's money in your DNA."

"Smart boy," said the camel creature, "I suppose you know that the Grilled Cheese Consortium is very interested in the possibilities of incest."

"Yes," replied Julius Baker, "I do know that. But I am not certain I know why."

"There are googleplex spacebucks in that syringe."

"That's very impressive," said Julius, trying not to let down his air of pimpish confidence. The fact that he ignored a sumo successfully shoving a giant flea into a volcano beneath him did this for him, though it did not occur to the master pimp.

"Wow!" exclaimed young Time Pimp.

"Wow indeed young man, wow indeed," said the camel tousling the boy's hair. The young pimp slapped the camel creature's hand.

"Ain't nobody touch a pimp without his permission!"

The camelbeast clapped.

"Yes, fantastic!"

Jetpacked knights floated down to drape a belt onto the triumphant Grand Sumo for his victory. The audience at all the other floating tables burst into applause. The pimps did not. A pimp applauds nothing.

"So what's this about?" asked Julius.

"We need someone to execute a job. A very important job. I believe your race is familiar with it and that's in the prophecies of The Game."

Julius poured another glass of water, transmuted it into cookie dough and nervously gulped it.

"I don't know how you know about that…"

"The Grilled Cheese Consortium is run by none other than Fank Toblerone. And Fank Toblerone is the richest being in all of time. Fank Toblerone is interested in changing history and creating a true sexual paradise. He believes executing The Vienna Job is a key to this. His analyst has told him that a pimp from the Baker bloodline would execute The Vienna Job."

Julius Baker slammed his fist on the table.

"That's a lie!" he screamed, "Nobody can do it! Nobody will ever do it!"

"But Mister Baker…"

"Get out of my sight!"

*1911*

Ka'ssen arrived naked in the Oval Office and got down on her knees on Theodore Roosevelt's desk. The rotund, burly, mustachioed president would have been frightened to see a naked blue woman manifest from nowhere on top of his desk were it not that he was Theodore fucking Roosevelt and knew nothing of fear. He kept a pet badger and he had finished a speech after getting shot. Not much of anything deterred Teddy.

"You gonna give me a nice rough ride, Mister President?" asked Ka'ssen, batting azure eyelashes at him.

"Bully!" said Theodore Roosevelt, whose biggest problem was no longer that someone was about to drive a giant purple Cadillac through the walls of the White House.

*4441*

Time Pimp had not expected for his shoes to lead him where they did. He had dreaded this year. He dreaded the company he was surrounded by and did not know how this awful and emotionally volatile species would respond. The pandas at the bar at first looked like they were ready for confrontation, until they took in from his manner of dress that he was not a person but a pimp and probably therefore not someone who would be that appropriate for slavery or their breeding pits. The pandas were prodigious drinkers and prodigious criers, as pathetic as they were wicked.

But one of them seemed sadder than all the others, a labcoated specimen whose goggled face was down on the bar, as beaten and defeated a creature as ever Time Pimp had ever seen. The panda did not look the type who would believe anyone would be happy to see him, which was a shame because Time Pimp found himself very relieved to see the panda that he had thought would be removed from the timestream.

"Hey, Professor! What's the good news?" asked Time Pimp.

The panda sat up.

"Excuse me?" Professor Panda slurred, "Excuse me, Playa. I don't believe we've met. I don't typically spend time with pimps and hos. Had a real rotten experience with a whore. Real rotten."

"You don't remember us?" asked a very disappointed Sister Cecilia.

The panda smiled lasciviously.

"Oh, I'd remember you, sugar," he said and fell off the stool flat onto his face.

"What happened to you?" said Time Pimp, "Damn, you're flat-out pathetic, Professor."

"Don't even get me started on pimps," he said, rising to

103

his feet and reaching up to poke Time Pimp in the chest with his clawed finger.

"Easy there, Pro-fessor, you don't want to say nothing you'll regret," said Time Pimp fingering the orgone cane. The panda snarled low. Time Pimp snarled too. He had once started to like the panda and thought he had misjudged him. He had missed the panda when he'd been murdered. Time Pimp was now wishing the panda would have stayed murdered and could oblige the panda's obvious death wish. Sister Cecilia sat down daintily on the stool beside Professor Panda. She placed her hand on his head, gently petting his soft fur. The panda's growling subsided, replaced by choking sobs.

"I loved Kjennen Ka'ssen! I loved her and she stole my PTSD."

Time Pimp shuddered.

"You built a PTSD?"

"Personal Temporal Sojourn Device. My crowning achievement. And she stole it, the whore. Now I'll never see her again unless I use my Planar Transport Signal Detector! And I'm too mad to do that!"

Time Pimp slapped his forehead.

"The fuck do you keep using that abbreviation?"

The panda broke into laughter.

"Holy shit. You thought I'd built a Perpetual Torment and Suffering Device? Shit. Those things are, they're…"

Professor Panda fell from his stool. He wiggled on the floor, too drunk to stand back up. Sister Cecilia got down on the floor, extending a hand to help the panda up. As she did, he pinched her firm ass and leaned in, attempting a kiss. She shoved him back to the floor. Kicked him in the rib.

"You're a fucking disgrace!" she snapped at him, "You're an insult to science!"

The panda struggled to his feet.

"What am I supposed to do? Use the device and find Ka'ssen?"

"No," said Sister Cecilia, "we're looking for her. You could give it to us and we could use it to track her through time and get the googleplex spacebucks she stole from us back."

"Okay," said Professor Panda, "we'll go to my lab and get it."

The three returned to the Professor's laboratory, a huge repository of gearspangled objects, steaming machines and beeping consoles. He handed Time Pimp a device that looked like a mobile phone from the eighties, huge, bulky and pink. Time Pimp put it up to his ear.

"1870," said a metallic voice, "The Black Saloon."

"Thanks, Professor," said Time Pimp, "I'll see you again." The panda nodded.

"I probably won't remember. I'm blackout drunk."

Time Pimp and Sister Cecilia rushed out to the Purple Cadillac, set it for the Wild West in 1870. It was barely a minute after they left when a camel wearing a grilled cheese sandwich appeared from a small, somewhat fishy-smelling timewomb.

"Professor Panda, I represent Fank Toblerone and the Grilled Cheese Consortium. We need a man like you."

*1920, Vienna*

"Oh my!" exclaimed the silver-haired Austrian woman, "Sigmund, you've grown into quite a man."

"He has," said Ka'ssen wrapping her hand around Freud's penis, "it's very impressive."

Freud nervously snorted a bit more coke.

"Ja. It is all for you, Mein Mother."

"And for me?" said Ka'ssen, lavender eyes meeting his, "surely there is enough to go around?"

"Ja, mein liebchen…"

Ka'ssen motioned Mrs. Freud closer. She took the old woman's hand, guiding it to the vaginal lips on her forehead. Nervously Mrs. Freud complied, inserting a trembling finger. The finger felt more than wetness. The finger felt static, heat, electricity, the constant movement of genital neurons. She felt body and mind become one and then let go, abandoning space, time and all other constraints to become someplace and something else. Kjennen Ka'ssen was the greatest fuck in history, giving not just body and essence but mind, and in

Ka'ssen's mind, Mrs. Freud found a place of pleasure, a palace of organic blue crystal, walls echoing with words, definitions, theorems, numbers and concepts. The palace was not simply made of crystal, but of Marxism, Grilled Cheese Dynamic Bussinomics, Taoism, paradox, embedded literatures and alchemical applications of the kama sutra, moving around caressing the fleshy subtle bodies at the speed of thought with the intensity of cunt contraction.

Sigmund, naked, hard, and triumphant, connected by the hand on his cock through a psionic conduit and his motherlust walked to the center of Ka'ssen's palace to meet his mother unafraid, to throw his arms around her and kiss her lips deeply. Though they had needed Ka'ssen to make this intimacy happen, they did not miss her or wonder where she was, as she had in fact become where they were. Freud and his mother guided themselves to the floor, which was warm and moist, covered in tiny moving hairs that tickled Mrs. Freud's back sensually, causing her pale, wrinkled skin to tingle and come to life. Sigmund grabbed one of the sagging teats that had once fed him, hungrily bringing to his mouth to taste what it had become.

He no longer felt he needed an invitation or that it was at all perverse to reenter the folds of the place that he came from. Sigmund Freud entered his mother, mouth full of ancient tit, and made love to the woman who had given birth to him inside the psychic vagina of the greatest prostitute in existence. He was tender in spite of the coke, wanting to make it last but knowing that in the palace of Kjennen Ka'ssen, there was no time, only thought and sex. Old though she was, she could wrap her legs around her son's back so that she might welcome him deeper into her secrets. Dry and loose though she was, he still savored the experience, thinking he had never had such a lover before and would never again.

From the place of tenderness, he moved onto pounding her furiously. It was as if each thrust was a stab into the wild heart of his many madnesses, his many abortive desires. He wondered if this could be the key to unlocking any madnesses, any abortive desires. He concluded that it had to be so. He felt a great deal of pity for anyone who lacked the capacity to coke up and fuck their mother, thinking that they would have to be fundamentally inhuman to miss the merit of such an experience.

He exploded with epiphany, he exploded with excitement, letting loose a great stream of lifeforce into old Mrs. Freud, knowing that in an odd way, he was conceiving himself and granting himself the freedom to be and do anything he chose. A man who could conceive himself would after all have no limits.

## 5054, Netzach

"Three rules, my son," said Julius Baker, sinking into the hot tub, putting one arm around Ka'ssen and one around a bikini-clad beauty whose transparent plastic skin revealed her organs, "three rules and you'll be all right."

"Shouldn't Death Pimp be here to hear this?"

Julius shook his head.

"Death Pimp is your Hater. Hater's gotta hate. This is Playa business, my son, my favorite son. This is shit for real pimps."

"I don't like that Death Pimp's gotta hate," said Time Pimp, "can't we help him not hate?"

Ka'ssen smiled.

"Such a caring boy. You should be very proud of your son. He'll grow up to be a great pimp one day."

"One day," said Julius, "but today, he doesn't get it. Playas gotta play the game, Haters gotta hate. There's no saving a Hater. He's gotta hate. But you're a Playa, so you get to hear the three rules. These rules are very important. First rule, don't touch another man's ho. Especially if that ho is Ka'ssen. Got it?"

Time Pimp nodded, though he didn't like it. Ka'ssen's smooth blue skin, large breasts and constantly bared forehead-pussy made her a great temptation to the boy and he wanted very much to grow up and use her like the ho she was. Time Pimp was very disappointed to hear that he would not be able to do this. Hopefully, Time Pimp would one day have hos of his own to touch. He was a Playa, so he surely would.

"Okay," said Time Pimp, "I won't touch Ka'ssen."

"Don't you worry, son, you'll have fine-ass bitches of your own someday."

"I hope so."

"I know so," said Ka'ssen, before putting her head underwater to suck Julius off.

"Second rule," said Julius as if the greatest prostitute in the universe was not sucking on his orgone, "always collect yo money. You can't not collect yo money. If you don't collect yo money then you ain't playin' the game right. And if you ain't playin' the game right, then there gonna be consequences."

"What kind of consequences?"

"That ain't important. What's important is that you obey the fucking rules and you play the game right."

"Yes, sir," said Time Pimp. He hoped he would never have to find out those consequences.

*1920, Vienna*

The monocled, mohawked, charcoal-suited woman extended a tray of Space Manticore milk grilled cheeses.

"You have performed optimally, Time Pimp and Kjennen Ka'ssen. The Vienna Job has gone better than we could have ever imagined. By which I mean it has actually been executed. We at the Grilled Cheese Consortium really didn't see that coming. Time Pimp, I think you might be Pimpking material. And Fank Toblerone agrees. He will be willing to personally endorse your bid for Pimpking."

Time Pimp's face wrinkled. He was not altogether certain why Fank Toblerone was still alive, but he did appreciate the thought of possibly becoming Pimpking. Julius Baker was up for Pimpking but his bid had been defeated. Time Pimp liked the thought of outdoing.

"That's right, Client, Time Pimp is the smoothest of all smooth pimp daddies. I am a wheeler, a dealer and a heart stealer and you'd best recognize!"

Time Pimp alchemized four cognacs and passed them around for a toast.

"To Time Pimp!" said the woman from the Grilled Cheese Consortium "The future Pimpking!"

"To Time Pimp! The future Pimpking! Recognize!"

Dispensing with cognac and delicious grilled cheese, the lady from the Grilled Cheese Consortium handed Time Pimp a syringe.

"As agreed upon, googleplex spacebucks. It has been a pleasure working with you, sir."

She shook Time Pimp's hand.

"The pleasure's all mine, like these googleplex spacebucks!"

And all present laughed as the lady from the Grilled Cheese Consortium disappeared into a small timewomb.

Ka'ssen bowed at Time Pimp's feet.

"Noble Time Pimp, you have done very well."

She kissed the right platform shoe in which her former pimp was now floating as a psychic octopus.

"Not only are you your father's son, but you might have surpassed him."

DON'T FUCK UP. The shoe octopus projected into his son's mind. BE CAREFUL.

"My dear Time Pimp, you are king. You are a master of men and you will see greatness. We have accomplished so much already…"

DON'T FUCK UP.

"Come kiss me, sweet Cecilia, come taste me. Come celebrate."

DON'T FUCK UP.

Sister Cecilia knelt beside Ka'ssen and their lips met. And soft and sultry as both the women were, it was pleasing to them. And so they kissed once more. Ka'ssen freed Time Pimp's orgone glowing bright with passion, a kingly sun illuminating the room. She worked it as she kissed Cecilia again, filling the nun with heat and excitement.

"Taste me," said Ka'ssen, and Cecilia did, her wet pink tongue entering the mind and sex of the great prostitute. And she traveled, vanished into the palace of the Blue Beast.

"Now," she turned to Time Pimp, "fuck me. Celebrate with us."

And the orgone slid into the mindcunt of the greatest of all prostitutes, the woman who had pulled off The Vienna Job and made him googleplex spacebucks. And it was beyond simple bliss. It was liberation from all things but itself, as the act that Time Pimp stood for was supposed to be. And it bore Time Pimp into itself, enveloping him in its reality.

Time Pimp and Sister Cecilia were alone and blissful in the palace of Ka'ssen the Blue Beast. They were not accustomed to making love. They desired to in this place and time but it was simply not them. So instead, they stared. They took in the scenery, they bathed in the ideas, theorems and concepts and wisdoms. They knew each other.

"There was nothing between him and me," said Cecilia, "I know you were jealous but it was different from that. He was a good man and he needed us."

"I know."

"And isn't that what being a pimp is about?"

Time Pimp laughed.

"Being a pimp is about getting paid."

A blue gingerbread house manifested on the floor, iced with erotic juices. Time Pimp tore some of the roof off, while Sister Cecilia grabbed a smiling blue gingerbread pimp and bit his head off.

"I don't think you believe that and I don't think any pimp does. He didn't think you believed that."

"I don't care what he thought. That punkass would've been nothin' without me."

Cecilia bit an arm off the gingerpimp.

"I know," she said, swallowing, "You did good, Mister Iscariot. He said the same thing. The guy still knew his shit though. And he knew that you saw something in this whole neighbor love and forgiveness thing."

"Don't get sappy, Miss Magdalene. I ain't above slappin' a bitch."

"I'm shaking in my six-inch heels." Cecilia rather

pointedly bit the remainder of the gingerpimp in half. They shared a laugh.

"It's complicated. I don't think The Game is simple. Pimpin' ain't easy. But maybe it's easier than some of the other shit out there."

Sister Cecilia sat down beside Time Pimp. She took his hand. Reached up and pulled down his shades. She had never seen his eyes before. She was startled to find that they were as big and pink and rabbit-like as Death Pimp's. Their eyes met for the first time ever and in them she saw a pain that she had always suspected was present. But beyond the pain, there was something she had never thought would be there. There was fear.

"Something's wrong with you. I felt it when you came to pick me up. It's like you've been through something and with you that could be anything. I don't know what kind of crazy shit happens to you when I'm not around."

"They hooked me up to it," he said, a tear sliding down his cheek, "and I felt responsible. Like I'd fucked up. And like all the shit that's supposed to be true isn't true anymore and I don't know what's supposed to be there instead."

"Like in Anhedonia when you found me."

"Yeah, like in Anhedonia. I think I'm in love with Sylvia. Like a bitch."

She kissed the tear from Time Pimp's cheek.

"I'm sorry."

"And she's dead. He killed her and it was my fault."

She took him in her arms and they sat there, enveloped in each other and the warmth of the palace of the Blue Beast. And Time Pimp cried. Like a bitch. Until he stopped. Until he felt nothing but the woman in his arms and the heat and the knowledge and the power and glory and intensity of the blue palace. And the complications felt simple.

Time Pimp and Sister Cecilia emerged from euphoria to find themselves again in Freud's office. Freud and his mother were asleep and spooning in the corner of the room, stinking of sweat, passion and the fluids of love. They were naked, blissful and as exhausted as two human beings could be without the danger of not waking up again. Time Pimp and Cecilia, substantially rose to their feet.

"She is really good," said Sister Cecilia, wiping pussy/brain juice off her lips. Time Pimp put on his pants, tucking his luminescence inside.

"She's the best ho there ever was."

"Where is she? Where is the syringe?"

"Uh oh."

*1978, Netzach*

Two orange-skinned men in purple velvet suits rushed into the room. They stood tall on octopus shoes, their eyes were concealed behind black shades and they held bearheaded golden canes in their hands. It didn't take more than a glance for Time Pimp to see that these gentlemen were obviously pimps. And they were obviously not happy. Julius Baker began sobbing. Time Pimp's Hater uncle began sobbing. Time Pimp dropped his orgone cane to the floor and threw his arms in the air.

"Attention, jiveass turkeys, we have come representing the Intergalactic Pimp Council," said one of them, "and we have come to arrest the pimp known as Time Pimp."

"You have got be kiddin' me," said Time Pimp, "I'm a stone-cold pimp daddy and I plays the game right!"

"No, son," said a crying Julius Baker, "you play the game like a punkass bitch. I gave you the three rules that day and you done broke them all. I wanted you to check yoself and you went and wrecked yoself!"

"You have failed to collect your money from your ho," said the other pimp, "you failed to get a client satisfaction, you gave a ho the cock without her begging for it, you caused a time travel paradox like a bitch and it looks like you gone and fucked your own mother. Time Pimp, you are literally a jiveass motherfucker. And you're gonna have to come with us."

"Dayum," said Time Pimp.

# THE
# TRIAL OF
# TIME PIMP

Soaking fully clothed in The Hot Tub of Justice high above Malkuth, Time Pimp was surrounded by the biggest Playas in the game; the red-scaled half-dragon Pyropimp Draconicus, Clavius Poindexter the bespectacled Pornbrarian Supreme of Netzach, the gigantic clockwork Steampimp of Alternate Albion 7 and Rex Domesticus, the half-terrier Dogpimp Supreme of Jupiter. Most impressive of all, looking smashing in his platinum tracksuit and sparkling under his diamond-studded afro was Pimpking Master Electrico, undisputed lord and master of the Pimp Council and Pimp of all Pimps. His word was law and it was said that his pimp slap could destroy buildings and turn mountains to dust. Under most circumstances, Time Pimp or any pimp at all would have been honored to soak in the tub with these gentlemen of distinction, Playas among Playas. But Time Pimp was here for business not pleasure and moreover, for punishment and not business. Few pimps had to meet the pimp council and those that did always returned thoroughly changed, often not at all for the better.

"Time Pimp," growled Pyropimp Draconicus, "you have been called here because of crimes against the game. Crimes of a serious nature. How do you plead?"

Time Pimp pulled down his shades, his pink rabbit-like eyes met with Pyropimp Draconicus' yellowish slit ones.

"Your honors, if it should please the court, I plead innocent. I committed no crimes against the game that were not committed to make the universe better for Playakind. I am a wheeler, a dealer, a man of distinction and a real high roller, and I request the court recognize."

"Court does not recognize," said Steampimp in his heavily metallic voice.

"I have done what I could to spread the love, play the game and get real paid. And if that ain't what pimpin's about, I don't know what is. Since I know there are no suckas and no lames among you, then I gots to say that Time Pimp is one smooth pimp. And deserves no punishments. I plead innocent."

The pimp council erupted into sinister laughter.

"Man," said Rex, "we was just fuckin' with you. Nobody

115

cares how the fuck you plead. If you're before the pimp council, we know you're fuckin' guilty so you just gotta wait while we decide how to punish your ass."

"All I wanted to was spread the love and get paid!" Time Pimp shouted, "this isn't fair!"

"Fair," said Clavius Poindexter adjusting his giant glasses, "does not enter into it. You failed. That makes you a bitch and a sucka and a lame and a stone-cold jiveass motherfucker. You will have to live with the consequences of your actions."

"Yes," said Pyropimp Draconicus, "you fucked up and there is only one possible punishment. The most severe at our disposal."

"I don't know," said Inscrutability Jones, "that seems severe to me. I don't think anybody deserves to go through that."

"Mr. Jones," said Pimpking Master Electrico, "you are new to the pimp council and I don't think you understand what it is to be a jiveass motherfucker like Time Pimp or to cry like a bitch or give up cock for hos or to touch another pimp's ho. None of these things are done, Playa. Except by Haters. And let's not even get started on what his Hater's gotten away with without gettin' his ass beat."

"He speaks the truth," said Clavius Poindexter, "Time Pimp's actions are inexcusable and could even have posed a danger to The Game itself. So before you go making yourself the fool, Mister Fool, I think you best recognize and learn respect before I pimp slap your lame ass."

"I second the need for Jones to learn respect before his lame ass is pimp-slapped," said Rex Familiaris, "Time Pimp has almost stepped into Hater territory. And I hate Haters."

Time Pimp folded his hands.

"Please, I didn't know the consequences. I didn't know she was my mother and I didn't know that I could put The Game in danger. I just wanted to pull off The Vienna Job."

"And you pulled off the Vienna Job," said Pimpking Master Electrico, "and like the jiveass motherfucker you are, you didn't even get your money. And there's consequences for that Time Pimp, motherfuckin' dire consequences. This court sees only one possible punishment for you. And it's bad."

Jones shrugged.

"Look man, Inscrutability Jones was on his own and he tried to reason but you done committed treason, my brother in pimpin'. So you gonna have to face the music."

"This court sentences you to the highest punishment a pimp can ever endure. Surrender your shoes. Your hos will operate autonomously from now on under the leadership of your top bitch. Time Pimp, you are no longer a pimp."

Time Pimp got out of the hot tub, which he had entered fully dressed. He pulled off his hat. And then with an anvil for a heart, he removed his treasured platform shoes from his feet, giving the octopi a silent telepathic goodbye.

"I'll miss you," said Time Pimp's uncle from his left shoe.

"I'll miss you," said Julius Baker from the right, "I love you son, but you have straight-up fucked the fuck up."

Time Pimp pulled off his shades, tears streaming down from his big pink eyes. He was crying like a bitch. He tossed the keys to The Purple Cadillac into the tub.

"Pimpin's all I know. What will I do now? Who will I be?"

Pimpking Master Electrico heaved a sigh as large as his orgone. Which was of course inordinately huge.

"Did I say I was fucking finished yet? No, I did not fucking say I was finished yet. Because you fucked the fuck up, not only are you stripped of pimp status, but…"

Time Pimp fell to his knees, crying even more like a bitch. He knew where this was going and this was the thing every pimp feared most. He had heard of only two pimps in history ever having had the sentence that was going to be called down on him. Neither had gone on to live happy lives.

"You can't do that to me! I'm Julius Baker's son! I was almost the Prince of Pimps. Come on, man, haven't you already done enough?"

"Almost!" shouted Clavius Poindexter, "And you could have almost become Pimpking. But you got cocky and you let bitches ruin your game and no pimp who lets bitches ruin his game becomes Pimpking. It is irrelevant now who your father was. He is ashamed of you, as are all pimps. You are one sadass jive turkey, Time Pimp."

"Please! I'll do anything!" This couldn't be happening. Someone would show up and fix this. He was having a nightmare. It was a misunderstanding. This could not have been happening to the mighty Time Pimp!

"Enough stalling," said Pimpking Master Electrico, "you are guilty of crimes against the game and you have been stripped of pimp status. And now that you have been stripped of that status, shoeless and crying like a little bitch, I pass sentence on you. You, Time Pimp are sentenced to life as a ho!"

*1066, Hastings*

Kjennen Ka'ssen discarded her third laser pistol of the chase. She'd had little experience shooting from horseback and the grunting, the slashing, the decapitations, the sundered shields and wanton brutality of the Battle of Hastings proved to be a huge distraction. Chainmailed helmeted warriors clashing blades and fighting for the future of England were not optimal conditions for shooting a dominatrix off a horse. There are few environments that provide such conditions.

Sister Cecilia was bearing down on her. Genghis Khan had a fast horse and Cecilia knew her way around a crop for obvious reasons. This was the fourth place in time and space that Cecilia had pursued Ka'ssen through since Time Pimp's arrest. She had wondered upon seeing her pimp arrested what she would do since she could not drive the Purple Cadillac and did not own any sort of time travel device herself. But Professor Panda arrived on the scene and once again came through. He had proven quite the useful ally.

"I can do this forever!" said Ka'ssen, "and there's no way you'll be able to catch up with me!"

Cecilia and the horse closed in. The dominatrix stood up on its back and with an acrobatic leap, landed right behind Ka'ssen on horseback. She hit a button on a small gadget dangling from her wrist and wrapped her left elbow around Ka'ssen's throat.

"Kjennen Ka'ssen, the Blue Beast, you are captured. You will be taken to Geburah and serve as a slave to me or to any clients that should require one. You will be punished for insubordination and any attempt to escape is considered a request to die. A request that will be honored. You are beaten."

Ka'ssen reached over to push the button on her PTSD. She tapped it. Nothing, tried it again, nothing.

"It's not working," she gasped, feeling faint from Sister Cecilia's elbow around her throat.

"Yeah. I have a PTSD."

"So do I."

Sister Cecilia smiled.

"Portable Time Skip Disruptor. Renders your PTSD inoperational. You're not going anywhere. Face it. You're mine, bitch."

*1898, Transylvania*

If music be the food of love, play on. Time Pimp wondered what it was that brought these words into his mind. Time Pimp wondered as well what it was that made him no longer Time Pimp, whether it was the feeling of lightness and litheness contrasted with a newly heaving chest which would have pleased him greatly were it not his own. Or was it the feeling of being outside in, a sensation that made him feel powerful but somehow deprived of the upper hand. He did not know the body fully or to be more precise, at all, and this was disconcerting. He would have sat where he was and reflected upon the situation, but it was cold and the violins in the distance seemed to be all that made sense. He missed his octopus shoes and their imperatives. They would have led him out of this situation. Maybe.

He was naked and it was cold and he was alone in the woods with only the sound of far off violins, clapping and dancing to guide him to something akin to civilization where he could figure out how to escape his new life as a ho. This did not seem like a very good place for the pimp council to send someone to transform them into a ho. He was most certainly a woman but he was not yet a ho. It was odd to him that he was making such a distinction. This was a dark forest primeval in the mountain pass where sinister owls stared out, their yellow eyes scrutinizing his new body that even he had not seen yet. Seldom had Time Pimp felt discomfort at something's gaze. This was a new feeling and he was not sure that he liked it.

His first experience in his new body was taxing it to its clumsy limits. He did not much know how to drive this new machine, but was nonetheless required by circumstance to run as fast as humanly possible, trying not to snap twigs under his bare feet and jumping over pits. He plucked brambles from his soft skin as she negotiated thorn bushes nicking and cutting him. He came at last to the source of music and she was relieved.

An encampment of dusky, dusty men playing violin, barefoot women in flowing skirts dancing, livestock, old women reading cards and tea leaves. Their clothes were smart but pragmatic, their faces weary but content, emitting an air of both cunning and wisdom. Gypsies. He liked these people. Since pimps spoke the language of love, she assumed the right words would come, but she was no longer a pimp. What came out was English, or as it was known on the Inner Planets of the Sefirot, "Galactic Standard."

"I am lost and naked and...."

Time Pimp stopped herself. She could not introduce herself has Time Pimp and had just declared herself lost and naked to an encampment of unfamiliar gypsies. This could not have been a good idea. There was nothing at all that could be said. She did not know who she was or what she would do now, only that she was at the questionable mercy of these strangers.

Speaking a language that was not Galactic Standard, an older man whispered back and forth with a head-scarfed old woman. They shouted, slapped each other. Hugged. Nodded. Went to a trunk and pulled out a flimsy but sumptuous low cut white dress. The old woman tossed it at Time Pimp.

"Put it on," she said in accented Galactic Standard.

She put on the dress. It was silky but tight and held up her breasts to the point of nearly spilling out from it. In spite of herself, she gave a compulsive curtsy of gratitude.

"Good manners," said the old man, "she will do."

The old woman approached her, sniffing her for some reason. Nodded.

"Virgin."

The statement was both true and comically ironic. This body had in fact not yet experienced penetration. It was new and fresh and though its inhabitant knew most everything there was to know about carnality she knew nothing about it from this context. She knew what brought women pleasure but not why it did. The word virgin felt ominous somehow. It struck her as both a compliment and pregnant with malice.

"You stay with me. Tomorrow we go to the castle."

She was generally fond of castles and the opulence they embodied, so these words were a relief. She slept on a straw mat in the dirty wagon beside the old gypsy woman. She dreamt of the smug blue face of Kjennen Ka'ssen laughing and eating an entire girljuice-iced gingerbread house, chewing with her mouth open and spitting bits of gingerbread everywhere. She woke up screaming, waking up the gypsy woman as well. The gypsy woman hugged her whispering calming words in Not Galactic Standard. Whatever these words were, they brought her a strange amount of comfort.

They traveled in the morning, horses clomping fast and frightened around tight corners of the frigid, mountain pass, until they came at last to a fortress, ancient, cyclopean, black as death, black as the space left behind by those you'll never speak to again. Its spires, odd gothic perfection towered high as if trying to rape the clouds for daring to dilute its wicked. As they approached this dread edifice, all of the wagons stopped, save the one carrying the woman who was once Time Pimp and the old woman, who pulled a pistol and a crucifix from under inside the straw mat.

The wagon came to a stop and the old woman pointed the pistol at the woman who was once Time Pimp.

"Please," she said to the old woman, now feeling very conscious of mortality, "I do not want to go there."

The old woman led her at gun point to a great wrought iron

door with a dragon engraved upon it. Holding her hands up, she complied and went to the door, which opened apparently of its own volition.

"Go in," said the old woman, backing away slowly, but still keeping her at gunpoint.

She complied and entered, the door slamming behind her the moment she did. The castle was stony, dark, labyrinthine, but just as she had followed the smell of music, she followed the smell of food down one of the hallways until she came to a gigantic table where fruits of all kinds and colors, vegetables and all manner of meats were laid out along with a decanter of wine and a note that said in Galactic Standard:

"Eat your fill. Sit and wait"

Having no other ideas and no notion of escape and a rumbling stomach, she complied, gourmandizing an immaculate cochinillo asado, slurping the juices from mangos, oranges and pomegranates and breaking up and devouring a basket of rolls. She ate until food grew frightful, but still did as the note said and sat and waited. And waited. And waited. She took a brief nap, awakened hungry enough to have a nibble of potato and then waited some more. All in all she sat for a good nine hours before she had company.

He was tall, around six foot four. Slender, but powerfully built. Handsome, middle aged and distinguished with a long equine face and a regal bearing. Yet as he sat down, there was an abruptness to him, like his gentile manners only masked an animal caged inside his imperious shape. He sat straight, dark eyes flashing pure authority, none of it moral. He spoke, his voice a booming baritone.

"I am Dracula," he said, "welcome to my house."

*5555, Netzach*

Colonel Troughton of the Grilled Cheese Consortium slammed down his fist upon the table.

"We've had enough!" he declared.

His camel-headed sandwich-suited cohort who had once at a sumo match on Yesod offered Julius Baker the Vienna Job

122

shook his head.

"You do not get to say such things. I will tell you when you've had enough."

Professor Panda's goggles extended as far as they could go and previously busy tinkering with something interrupted their argument. It had been going back and forth like this for over an hour. Troughton had had enough, yes, but his colleague felt that only he could decide how and when someone had had enough. This was a stalemate that could be nigh impossible to resolve.

"The fact of the matter is that it is in Fank Toblerone's hands and Fank Toblerone condones my giving Sister Cecilia the device so that she can find Ka'ssen."

"And our googleplex spacebucks!"

"And what concern is it of yours who has googleplex spacebucks?" asked the camelman. "The job was done and paid for. It doesn't matter who has that money and you certainly don't want the likes of Kjennen Ka'ssen having it!"

"Hmmph," snorted Professor Panda, "and why the hell not? She's brave, charitable, and upstanding and she's strong enough to run the bondage convent at Geburah. She'll find something good to do with that money."

"We are the Grilled Cheese Consortium," said the charcoal-suited mohawked woman, "we are not concerned about the dynamics of responsibility, fiscal or otherwise."

"We are concerned," said a gigantic stapler who toddled on cloven hooves, "about control. And we have lost control of googleplex spacebucks and The Vienna Job did not prove to be the coup that Fank Toblerone thought it was."

"Toblerone," said Colonel Troughton, "has made some questionable decisions in the past."

"I don't know what," said Professor Panda, sketching out a slot machine that he could fill with leeches, "I have never seen Fank make a questionable decision as long as I've known him."

"You are new," said the camel, "to the Grilled Cheese Consortium. There is much you do not know about us and our dealings."

It was almost as if on cue that they appeared, the pink

spirals. The hundred pink spirals. It was almost as if on cue that the latex covered thugs of The Morality Front emerged from all of these miniature timewombs. Firing hot latex into the flared giant nostrils of the camel from their condom-armored hands, they stood silent as he struggled to breathe and ran about the room, the inside of his phallic snout sizzling and constricting. The camel fell.

Troughton reached for martian disintegrator, taking aim at a cultist in front of him, but failing to notice that a time womb had materialized behind him and from it another one of the dispassionate condomed zealots was emerging to place a hand over his mouth and melt bullets of malleable plastic down his throat, constricting his air. Choking. The Morality Front was all about choking and of course never had problems leaving a roomful of bodies behind.

Ten of them grabbing the stapler's mouth like a great ape wrestling a tyrannosaurus rex, they pulled on it, bending his body backwards and snapping the two parts in half, revealing to the room his innards, a magazine of staples that would forever be unspent. Unspent. The Morality Front was all about unspent. And if they could take pleasure, the one of the few things that they would take pleasure in is the glorious concept of Unspent.

With a flurry of ugly, dispassionate kicks and punches, they brought the charcoal suited mohawked woman to the floor, severing her ties to life with an onslaught of beatings. These beatings were without rage, not crimes of passion but crimes of sexless violence. The Morality Front was all about sexless violence, one of the highest pillars of their ideology, brought down from their loveless pope. She and three others in the Consortium died on the floor of the corporate office, taken by faceless men.

Professor Panda had forgotten his PTSD. And his PTSD. He could have sent them back through time or sent himself elsewhere, but he had attended the meeting with only the plans, his goggles and sundry small parts. He was confused, thinking he should feel that he was about to die but having an almost cosmic certainty that this was not the moment and that he had an almost frightful amount of living left to do. But that couldn't be right, since three of them were bearing down on him.

A time womb opened and out stepped a tall, brunette, shapely female cadaver, neck held together by fused latex stitches. He could swear he recognized her from history books as the authoress and madwoman Ayn Rand. But this could not be so, just as his feeling that he was not about to die could not be so. A tape recorder was hanging from her neck. Imprecisely reaching out a dead finger, she hit "play."

A voice that Professor Panda did not like at all spoke to him.

"Greetings Professor. I have sent my proxy to offer you a job. I wish I could say that you had the option of declining said offer but I cannot. You will take it or you will endure eternities of rape and torture until I reanimate your corpse to pimp it out to the sickest creatures in the universe. Come with Ms. Rand, you have work to do, Professor."

*1898, Transylvania*

Four days had she been chained up in the dungeon. Four days alone in the dark and they were coming for her, fangs and gossamer, pallor and hate and lust. Skin almost luminescent, the only shapes that could be perceived in this dank, terrible place, they had teased, cajoled, molested and bitten her and not just for their sick pleasure. She knew about vampires. On Netzach, when she was Time Pimp, she'd had a couple vampires in her stable since a lot of clients were into that. He himself had gotten many a fanged orgonejob from undead hos, but the woman who was once Time Pimp certainly did not relish being at their mercy, and if she did ever regain pimp status and use of orgone, then never again would a vampires be permitted any kind of erotic privilege. Vampiresses and Kjennen Ka'ssen. They would all pay.

These thoughts made life in the dungeon somewhat easier. But not by much. She did not know how she would become a pimp again and if she would be able to escape or die before becoming a vampiress herself. The movement in the shadows of the dungeon confirmed that this was quite unlikely. Pale shapes in wispy white dresses clinging to their voluptuous bodies revealed themselves, assailing her with their cruel laughter and flashes of their ivory fangs.

"Are you ready, my sweet one?" asked the blonde, "Do you want to be forever lovely?"

"Yes," sighed the brunette, "we'll be such dear friends."

"Do not worry, sisters dear," said the redhead who was the cruelest, tall as a man and mean as a snake, "she simply has no choice in the matter."

The three vampiresses giggled together. The woman who was once Time Pimp felt like crying. Like a bitch. Which was appropriate, since she was now, by Time Pimp's definition, a bitch. A lowly ho chained to a dungeon wall in nineteenth century Trannsylvania and about to be turned into a vampire.

Elsewhere in the castle, Sister Cecilia, Sherlock Holmes (the real one who was most decidedly not Death Pimp), Watson and their friend Professor Van Helsing (an affable but austere gentleman with great taste in smoking jackets who could have been Holmes' twin) were searching for the diabolical count, who, having had all of his coffins in the village below located and destroyed, had fled to his lair, not knowing that Holmes and Watson had of course had the foresight to come in and consecrate the coffin the previous day.

"Let's split up," Holmes suggested, "we'll cover more ground that way."

"Brilliant, Holmes!" said Watson exuberantly, "masterful tactic!"

Sister Cecilia lit the dark castle with her warm, once rare smile.

"This has been such great fun," she said, tearing up, "thank you, Sherlock, thank you, Professor. This helps keep my mind off of Time Pimp."

"You have been a brave, loyal companion," said the Professor, "sweet Cecilia, it has been a pleasure embarking on this campaign against the living dead by your side."

Holmes and Watson headed for the library, deducing that

Dracula would not be there and they would have some time to make out and could claim some of the glory without risking being vampirized. Professor Van Helsing dashed down a hallway. For a middle aged man Van Helsing was awfully fond of running and jumping. Sister Cecilia decided to take a different approach, assuming a vampire would put a coffin someplace dark, so descended the stairs to the dungeon.

Upon descending the stairs, she found a blonde, a freakishly tall redhead and a short brunette preparing to attack a tall, emerald-eyed blonde who had been chained to the dungeon wall.

"Stop!" cried Sister Cecilia.

The vampiresses turned, baring fans and unison and preparing a fearsome charge that would have ended the life of a lesser combatant. But they were facing Sister Cecilia, who firmly presented the crucifix from around her neck.

"Back, fiends! You will not feast on this innocent girl today!" she shouted, leaping forward with her cutlass and in a single triumphant slash taking the blonde's head from her shoulders as she had once done to the similarly vampiric Ayn Rand. She pounced upon the brunette, stabbing her in the heart, withdrawing the blade and taking the vampiress' alabaster head. The redhead, skulking through the shadows, got behind Sister Cecilia and therefore no longer under the influence of the crucifix.

The woman who was once Time Pimp felt an explosion of affection and relief at the sight of Sister Cecilia. He wished to shout out that she was Time Pimp, but could not, as she was now no longer Time Pimp but a ho and making such claims was just not possible. But as light as the sight of Sister Cecilia had made her heart, she panicked at the red-haired vampiress sneaking up on the nun, afraid that she would lose her dear friend as soon as she reclaimed her.

But this fear quickly proved itself unfounded as Sister Cecilia reached into the bodice of her habit and tossed a tiny vial at the creature sneaking up on her, causing its skin to sizzle. She mule-kicked the vampiress in the knee, causing the dazed burning creature to stumble, tumbling to the ground.

The nun followed the red-haired vampiress down, diving on top of her, stabbing her in the heart three times before making the coup de grace and severing the monster's head.

She then turned her attention to the woman who was once Time Pimp, cutting her chains and releasing her.

"So," said Sister Cecilia, "who are you and how the fuck did you get down here?"

"Well…"

"Know what? Let's get into the light," said Sister Cecilia, taking the woman by the hand and practically dragging her upstairs, where it was better lit. Sister Cecilia gave the former prisoner a once over. She liked what she saw. Tanned, athletic, blonde hair, distinguished nose, emerald-green eyes, long legs and a nice pair of breasts supported well by the dress. Although she had never seen this woman before and this woman did not look like who she actually was, for some reason Sister Cecilia felt she knew her.

"So," said Sister Cecilia, "who are you and how the fuck did you get down there?"

"I'm…" Time Pimp attempted to say that she was Time Pimp. She swore she had chosen to utter the words Time Pimp. But what came out of her mouth was different.

"I'm a dirty stupid ho."

"Hmm."

"I mean, that's not at all what I mean. What I meant to say was that I'm a dirty stupid ho."

Again, the words selected, loaded into the chamber of Time Pimp's mind and yet they could not come to pass. Instead of a flag that read "Bang" there was instead the statement that she was a dirty stupid ho, a statement that burned itself into her mind, repeating to her that it was true, challenging all that she had known of being a pimp and exercising so much of her personal power.

Sister Cecilia slapped the ho across the face.

"Have some respect, whore. This is a dignified position. You don't have to talk like a fucking slut."

Sister Cecilia slapped Time Pimp across her face. The woman once Time Pimp shuddered, taken aback and discombobulated. Instinctually the woman replied with a slap. It came out light, slow, the work of someone who had relied upon slapping technique and preternatural slapping powers to get their slapping done. It was weak, a disappointment. The slap barely grazed the nun who gave back what she had received in the blink of an eye. Time Pimp stumbled, tumbled, fell.

Surprised Time Pimp got to her feet again. She had taught Sylvia to add Pimp Fu techniques to her existing combat training and to her natural inclinations. Time Pimp felt almost as proud to be on the receiving end of Cecilia's ferocity as he did disappointed. Cecilia was again wearing the smile that used to come so rarely.

"Hmm," you are willful and insubordinate. You might be strong enough to be one of mine. Yes, I think you'll go with me to Geburah."

Before anything else could be said, Count Dracula came running through the room and right behind him the very well dressed and determined Professor Van Helsing. And behind him running slower were Sherlock Holmes and Watson. Cecilia joined up with Holmes and Watson and with her came the woman once Time Pimp, who did not want to leave the nun's sight in spite of the difficulties that were sure to ensue from sticking with her, the likes of which he did not even begin to understand.

They ran into the diningroom to find that Count Dracula and Professor Van Helsing's chase had led them to the top of the long supper table. Dracula, eyes glowing red, great fangs out was lunging for the Professor. The smoking-jacketed gentleman was undeterred even as the snarling devil was about to finish him. He had been brave enough to chase the vampire into the room, so was not going to die a coward. Grabbing two kitchen knives, he crossed them focusing heavily and with all of his conviction presenting the makeshift cross at the vampire who was surprised to find himself relenting. The vampire inwardly cursed the ubiquity of his Achilles heel. He compounded the humiliation by stepping into a pot of cranberry shot.

Sherlock Holmes drew his trusty revolver, pointed at a nearby window and squeezed off a shot.

"Brilliant, Holmes!" cried Watson as the window shattered.

"Dawn come and take you!" shouted Professor Van Helsing.

The vampire did not need to turn around. There was no good that it could possibly do him. Had Holmes and Van Helsing been bluffing, it wouldn't have mattered much. But they were not. The first rays of the sun were indeed being born in the sky. These rays came together, touching the vampire, cutting, burning, and negating. The count's cape, dark suit, face and flesh were soon aflame and the flames soon out, leaving instead only ashes of the ancient master vampire.

"Is it over?" asked Watson.

"For now," replied Professor Van Helsing with cautious optimism, which was really the best attitude one could present when hunting down and disposing of immortal predators like Count Dracula.

Sister Cecilia bounced up and down. It was appreciated by all.

"That was so great! We killed Dracula!"

Van Helsing placed Sister Cecilia's hand in his and kissed it.

"My dear, I think we all can say that we could not have done it without you and your swordsmanship and your passion and your fast horse. Sister Cecilia, you are a treasure."

Cecilia grinned big.

"Well, aren't you sweet, Professor?"

"Speaking of sweetness," said Holmes lighting his pipe, "I deduce that you found the young lady in the white gown in the dungeon. From the slight smell of patchouli and the straw and the strong smell of pack animals, it seems as if she has been traveling among gypsies. From her constant blinking, one can tell she has been in the dark while now. But I cannot tell who she is."

"Brilliant, Holmes!" cried Watson, "How do you do it?"

"Well," said Sister Cecilia, "it appears that for once I have a leg up on the great Sherlock Holmes. But I'm afraid I don't know all that much more than you do. All I know about this girl is that she is a filthy whore."

"Hmm," said Holmes, "A ho, you say? How delightful.

And fortunate considering your own line of work. I do hope this exercise has granted you some of the confidence you'll need to handle Time Pimp's affairs during his absence."

"If she's a whore," said Watson, "We should stay clear of her altogether. You have been spending all too much time around whores as of late, my dear Holmes."

"You're just jealous, Watson. This young lady seems like a perfectly clean and skillful ho."

"Thank you, sir," said the woman once Time Pimp, a little confused to see Sherlock Holmes and traumatized from his encounter with Death Pimp who had worn the guise of the consulting detective when last they clashed.

Sister Cecilia mussed the woman once Time Pimp's hair. Kissed her forehead.

"Such good manners. Why don't you show Sherlock Holmes some courtesy. Suck Holmes' cock."

How dare she! His ho was telling him that he was to suck a cock like a bitch! Time Pimp did nothing like a bitch. Time Pimp was a stone cold pimp daddy, a man of distinction and a real big spender.

"I don't suck no cocks," said Time Pimp…yes, Time Pimp. He did not have to act like this bitch he had become. Time Pimp wasn't a bitch.

The smack jangled her senses. The second one loosened her brain.

"I rescued you for vampires and you are most certainly a filthy whore," said Sister Cecilia, "and filthy whores in my company do as I say because I am top bitch, do you understand? I am abbess of the Domvent of Geburah, slayer of the former Mother Superior of Anhedonia. You are mine and you will do as I tell you."

Another slap.

"Now suck Holmes' cock."

And so the bitch once Time Pimp opened her mouth and sucked Sherlock Holmes' cock. Like a bitch.

"I like you," Sister Cecilia whispered into her ear, "you are lovely and willful."

## 2117, The Black Saloon

"You know," said Longitude Browning, the beret'd and vested skinnyjeaned Hater to Clavius Poindexter, "I think we might suck."

"Agreed," said Flambeus Watershed, whose top half was that of a man and his bottom half was covered in light scaling, rather underwhelming, half-dragon traits, "none of us are very good at what we do at all. Sometimes I wish I was a pimp."

"Death Pimp is good," said Mustachewax Phosphor, the bemonocled, pigriding nemesis of Steampimp from the top of his dieselpig, "Death Pimp is a great Hater. So not all Haters suck."

"Maybe Death Pimp is too good," said Assault Weapons Cat, Rex's giant cat Hater, as he fired an AK-47 at the ceiling for no discernible reason beyond his pride that his new robot hands allowed him to finally fire an assault weapon.

"Yeah," Longitude agreed, "I'm not sure I wanna go as far as Death Pimp does with the hate. I know Haters gotta hate, but we don't have to be psychos about it. I mostly like to trip Clavius up with feminist blogging and spreading rumors that he has gonorrhea."

"I like your blog," said Mustachewax, "you make some salient points about pornography. It's icky and exploitative."

"I think your blog sucks," said Assault Weapons Cat, "and I think you suck."

Flambeus clapped politely.

"There you go. Haters gotta hate, don't we?"

"I don't know if we have to hate each other," Mustachewax chimed in.

"It's all very ambiguous," said Longitude, "I think we should stick together. So I like these meetings. It's much less stressful than feminist blogging."

The longhidden door of The Black Saloon flew open, kicked in by a condomarmored adherent of the Morality Front. The adherent had of course not come alone, bringing with him about a dozen of his comrades. For most, this would be a disturbing sight, but these were Haters.

"Hmm," said Assault Weapons Cat, "looks like Death Pimp has come to pay us a visit."

"Good," said Flambeus, "I miss Death Pimp. He never goes to these things."

The room's goodwill faded when Professor Panda entered.

"Aah!" screamed Longitude, "A panda!"

"Uh oh," said Mustachewax, "I'd heard a rumor that the Wealthy Dowager's Supper Club was eating Death Pimp forever at the end of time. Looks like he's been replaced by a panda. We're in some trouble now."

"Don't worry," said Assault Weapons Cat, "I got my hands just for this occasion..."

The resplendently evil, mitred, robed form of Death Pimp entered The Black Saloon, stopping everything cold and confusing all present.

"You all suck. You are abject failures and will never do better. You will always lose The Game to the pimps that oppose you," he declared, "and you make me sick."

Flambeus applauded the Grand Etharch.

"Yeah! It's so good to see you, Death Pimp."

"I wish I could say the same, you mewling, impotent, cowardly little bitches. But I cannot. It saddens me that you are fellow Haters, but I feel an obligation to the hate, so I must include you in my plans."

"We're glad to help," said Longitude, "but what's the plan?"

"Well, for starters, we're going to murder the pimp council with a Perpetual Annihilation and Impurification Device."

*Geburah*

Public executions on most planets are generally not a beautiful thing to behold. They tend to be spectacles of cruelty, mercilessness and voyeuristic perversity. This was not so on Geburah, where execution had been practiced in public from the beginning, before society had created a voyeuristic demand for them. The general purpose of executions on Geburah was an instructional one. Those who performed public executions

133

on other planets were often self-deluded into thinking that what they did was always morally instructive. On Geburah, this was actually so.

As the woman once Time Pimp walked the streets of Geburah's capital, she took great joy in witnessing Geburah's executions. This was not out of a love of violence (though pimps loved violence), but out of an appreciation for one of the most beautiful of the universe's legal systems. Geburah had attained mastery of violence and its purposes and was peerless in demonstrating these. The nuns of Geburah for lesser criminals would administer graceful but savage beatings.

One such tall, ebony-skinned nun was beating a microwave headed cyborg's buttocks raw with a cane, so hard that some of the skin was peeling off, white and flaky under the expert savagery of the nun that punished him. She had a smile on her face, not of sadistic glee, but of meditative focus and contentment and of pride in her particular task, which was of course to the nuns of Geburah a sacred one.

When she ceased caning, she freed him from the stocks and he stood up. She hugged him tightly, rubbing her face against his door.

"Thank you," he spelled out in green digits, before taking his leave of the nun, stepping upon a teleportation platform to carry him back home a better, wiser citizen brutalized with a desire to improve his life and consciousness. This was an impressive spectacle, but only a minor one in Geburah. The small beatings were routine and simple and did not gather crowds from other worlds as the greater triumphs of Geburah's laws did.

In the town square of Geburah's capital, hundreds of bodies had nooses around their necks, some humanoid, others specially designed for beings with shorter, cybernetic or nonexistent necks, made instead to squeeze the being to death with mechanical restraints. Mantis people, weresharks, cyborgs, minotaurs, headless dwarves and other species were all prepped for execution. This by itself would be a spectacle of cruelty and the only pride that Geburah would deserve would be having the ingenuity to kill anything. But these executions were beautiful, special and moving displays.

Why? Because among the crowd in the front row were the criminals themselves, consciousness separated from body so they could witness and comprehend their executions. They felt the noose, they felt the despair that had inflicted and they felt the pain that was being inflicted upon their bodies. As peerlessly lovely nuns pulled the levers to hang their corporeal forms, their psyches and souls learned the depths of suffering.

After a moment kneeling in front of, praying for and addressing their bodies, the psyches and bodies were reintegrated, observer and body once again together to fully process what had happened. This was met with howls of pain and torment, crying and trembling. The nuns cut them down, embracing them as they had the beating victims, but doing so harder, peppering them with kisses, lying them down upon the ground and rubbing their embattled and traumatized bodies all over with massage techniques they had learned from the pimps and prostitutes of Netzach, bringing the once dead to peace and orgasm, their cries going from screams of pain to exhalations of joy. When they were done, the criminals embraced their executioners, offering them kisses, hearty thanks and apologies.

"We are all sorry, we were all wrong. We thank you for your mercy and your understanding, goddesses."

"You are not forgiven," the nuns replied universally, "You will have no more chances."

And solemnly, the criminals would be teleported back to their worlds of origin where they would universally go on to be loving and caring citizens who committed no further crimes. They had no reason for guilt, hate and self-loathing and no reason to sin again. This was why the woman who was once Time Pimp took such pleasure in watching Geburah's executions and harbored more respect for Sister Cecilia than he would ever have dared to let on. As executioners went, Cecilia had no equal.

The crowds applauded the return of Sister Cecilia with a new ho and her sisters ran to her, kissing her boots and offering warm hellos, which Sister Cecilia returned with the same kindness and enthusiasm with which they were given in the first place. It took a great while to navigate the town square crowd before reaching the ten-thousand stairs that led up to the Convent of Geburah, stairs that had been built to insure not only the health and discipline of the nuns but also to make sure that the convent would only be approached in earnest.

The new legs of the woman once Time Pimp ached by the time she reached the top, wondering if she would be able to walk right again. She wanted to complain but knew better. She was in the hands of Sister Cecilia and Sister Cecilia took discipline seriously and made those who did not pay dearly. The woman once Time Pimp was now on Geburah and on Geburah, she too would have to take discipline seriously whether she liked it or not. Sister Cecilia would probably end up making it so that she did not like it.

At the top of the stairs, the woman once Time Pimp was greeted by a statue of himself. At the base was inscribed "Thank you for saving the day." The woman once Time Pimp felt very sad seeing those words. All he had really done was free Sister Cecilia from her condom cocoon and she decided everyone else needed freedom. He did not save the day and he didn't like thinking of himself as someone who did. He was a pimp and a pimp got paid. That's what was important. Getting paid. At least it was. Now what was important was serving as a ho because he had been a bitch and failed.

Passing through the convent door on which there was engraved a woman on her knees, he felt a cold blast of solemnity hit her in her heart and between her legs. To call the convent austere would be an understatement. The walls and floors were a color grey that had been specifically created in Geburah's discipline lab to discourage idleness and sloth. Sister Cecilia took hold of the woman once Time Pimp by her hair.

"Get down on your knees," she ordered, "now."

"I don't…"

Sister Cecilia pulled hard.

"Did I fucking stutter? I said get down on your knees."

The woman once Time Pimp did, but did so hesitantly.

Sister Cecilia walked ahead coolly dragging the woman once Time Pimp behind her with a shocking strength. The woman once Time Pimp instinctually pulled against it, but found this an excruciating mistake. She did not like being led around but if she resisted then the consequences would be quite dire.

Sister Cecilia stopped, opening the door to a chamber made almost entirely of this gray. A stone slab with a single pillow upon it lay in the corner of the room. Sister Cecilia pressed a keypad on the wall.

"You have been a bad girl. Wait here for three years."

And Sister Cecilia took her leave of the woman once Time Pimp leaving her to contemplate her insubordination.

*The Hot Tub of Justice*

"Boy," said Draconicus, "we sure showed that bitch Time Pimp."

"Hell yeah," said Rex, extending his paw for a high five, which Draconicus had no qualms about giving, "can you imagine that little bitch being Julius Baker's son?"

"Julius Baker wasn't no thing," said Clavius Poindexter downing a glass of cognac, "he talked a big game, but he had a little bitch for a son."

"I'll drink to that," said Pimpking Master Electrico, raising a glass of cognac, "to overrated straight up bitches who can't teach their kids no respect."

"Fuck you," said the voice of Julius Baker, psychically projected from the shoes by the side of the Hot Tub of Justice, "you're nothin' but a bunch of Haters."

"You can't call me a Hater!" shouted Pimpking Master Electrico, "you're dead!"

"Better than bein' a jiveass turkey," projected the shoe octopus.

The argument could have escalated if it weren't for the rippling and the scent of time wombs opening all around the hot tub. The slight sensual scent of dozens of them pervaded the air and filled it with crackles of energy and raw potential. The baffled pimps did not even have time to emerge from the water before a couple hundred condomclad Morality Front foot soldiers shambled out from the places between space and time. Followed afterwards by Assault Weapons Cat, Flambeus, Longitude and Mustachewax all cackling ominously.

"Shiiit," said Pimpking Master Electrico, "looks like we got Haters. Good thing you're all a bunch of punkass bitches!"

Pimpking Master Electrico gasped, eating his words when Professor Panda appeared holding a remote control.

"Fuck! It's a panda!" shouted the Pimpking.

"I'm sorry," said Professor Panda anemically, "he made me make it."

The arrival of Death Pimp with a strange orb floating around his head clarified the situation and filled the hot tub with panicked excrement. The pimps looked back and forth at each other, then at the Haters, then at Professor Panda, then at Death Pimp and then at the object floating around him. They began to cry like little bitches.

"Please," said Pimpking Master Electrico, "don't do this. We'll give you anything. We'll give you your own pimp shoes. It will be the first time a Hater had them."

"Too little," said Death Pimp, "and too late. But you gentlemen should be grateful, you're about to achieve the aim and the name of the game, you know that? You're about to get PAID."

"Hnhhh," gasped Clavius Poindexter, "shit, that's a Perpetual Annihilation and Impurification Device!"

"Yeah," said Longitude, crossing his arms defiantly, "you're damn right. And you're about to get PAID."

"He just said that," Mustachewax reminded him.

"I'm sorry," said Professor Panda. There were black circles under the black circles under the panda's eyes and the white in his fur had become a dingy yellow color. He looked about half dead.

"Hit the button, panda," ordered Death Pimp, "betray reality."

The panda closed his eyes and hit the single red button on the remote. Tentacles of energy manifested from the side of the floating ball. The wiggled, trembled and hissed with power. A single sad eye appeared on the center of the sphere, looking on at the horrors it was about to cause. The PAID was very much alive and very much in torment. A torment that forced it to lash out, extend and whip Draconicus with one of its tentacles.

The energy tentacle burrowed into the dragon man's being, squeezing, yanking, dragging it backwards in time, depriving Draconicus of every moment of his life until at last it was no more. There was never a human/dragon hybrid in the hot tub and there never would be unless Flambeus decided to jump in. But he of course did not, since he was a Hater. The next tentacle lashed out at Rex, violating, probing, and dragging the super-evolved dog out of existence. The eye at the center of the PAID looked disgusted but it carried on, a machine of organic self-loathing that unmade all that it touched. Steampimp. Clavius. Inscrutability Jones. Pimpking Master Electrico. All dragged by the tendrils transported through time and outside of being.

In a disgusting, short anticlimactic amount of time, The Intergalactic Pimp Council was no more. The Haters exchanged dirty looks and unspoken questions. Professor Panda sobbed into his paws. Assault Weapons cat emptied his clip into the air. PAID emitted a buzzing, whining noise. It was the robotic equivalent of a wounded animal begging for death. The Haters with the exception of Death Pimp exchanged another round of dirty looks and unspoken questions.

Then they hugged. They bounced up and down. They laughed and smiled and reveled in their freedom. Without the Intergalactic Pimp Council around, the Haters found it very difficult to come up with anything to hate.

"This is going to be great," said Mustachewax whose monocled was fogged up with tears of joy, "we got PAID. We won the game."

"Yeah," said Assault Weapons Cat, "this is the start of something really beautiful. Death Pimp totally came through for us."

"I love Death Pimp," said Longitude, "he's the best."

"Yeah," said Flambeus, turning to Death Pimp, "you're the man, dawg."

"I do what I can," replied Death Pimp, "Haters gotta hate."

"Not anymore we don't!" exclaimed a smiling Assault Weapons Cat.

The Haters laughed together and high-fived, with the obvious exception of Death Pimp, who they figured was not particularly fond of high-fives. They were quite right in this assessment. The last time Death Pimp was high-fived, it ended in headshots, reanimation and extremely degrading acts of necrophilia broadcast through the Morality Front Brainband network so that nobody would get the idea of trying to high five the Grand Etharch ever again.

"So, Death Pimp, what are we gonna do now?" Longitude asked.

"Yes, I was wondering the same thing myself," said Mustachewax, "we don't have any Playas to hate. Except for Time Pimp, wherever he is."

"Are we going to hate Time Pimp now?" asked Assault Weapons Cat, "I guess that's enough Playa for us all to hate."

"No," said Death Pimp, "we are not all going to hate Time Pimp now."

"Great," said Flambeus, "I really appreciate the opportunity to take a break from hate. It's really stressful."

Death Pimp shook his head.

"You're not going to hate Time Pimp because you're all pathetic. You were given the sublime gift of hate and squandered it on cowardice, self indulgence, and the dubious pleasures of being a casual nuisance to beings I eradicated with the push of a single button. A button, I might add, that my panda friend is about to push."

The Haters did not get a chance to flee. Like their pimp counterparts, they could not escape the tendrils of PAID's judgment and hatred of its foul purpose. They could not escape the power of Perpetual Annihilation. Within minutes of Death Pimp's arrival, pimp council and counterparts alike had been erased from history itself. For someone who had this specific vendetta instead of a loud, grotesque carousel of vendettas, this would have engendered closure and satisfaction. Alas, concepts like "closure" and "satisfaction" were generally wasted upon Death Pimp.

The Grand Etharch thought now of his father. Julius Baker had disapproved of, snubbed and beaten Death Pimp, although in reality Time Pimp, being raised by a pimp, had not fared that much better. But Death Pimp did not see if this way. The Player/Hater dichotomy was a powerful force in pimp culture and a destructive one for Death Pimp in particular. Julius Baker would be a good next target for his vendetta. And Ka'ssen. Death Pimp had always found it funny that Time Pimp had grown up with such a furious crush upon Kjennen Ka'ssen and never been perceptive enough to determine that she was their mother.

And then Time Pimp. Time Pimp was the big one of course. He really hated Time Pimp, since it was not just his station to do so but also his passion. He was very excited about Perpetually Annihilating Time Pimp. He had found out from the glittercloud of Yod that Time Pimp was being sentenced at the Hot Tub of Justice. It seemed that either he had gotten the chronal coordinates wrong or the Hot Tub had some kind of effect on time bending around it. He wondered if annihilating The Pimp Council had undone their sentence on Time Pimp, who he had just missed it seemed. The annihilation had in fact not worked this way. As evidence of this, the familiar platform shoes and orgone cane that had been doffed tubside were still lying about, useless to anyone.

Death Pimp could have asked Professor Panda why this was so, but he did not as the answer would no doubt be very scientific and boring to pretty much anyone. Death Pimp instead decided he would grab Julius Baker and then Ka'ssen, then he would track down Time Pimp and Perpetually Annihilate him, whatever that actually meant.

*Geburah*

Viola was crushed beneath the weight of passing days. She could not count them since there were no calendars and there was no light at all in her cell and she could not speculate since extended time travel often made these things either moot or difficult to figure out. What she knew was that it had been a long time or at the very least a long time to be alone in a cell with nothing but a stone slab to sleep on and bowls of flavorless gruel teleported in. Pimps did not do much waiting. They gave orders and made hos wait. Olivia was waiting. Like a ho. Like a bitch. And she cried, once again, like a bitch.

Why had Sister Cecilia rescued her and brought her to Geburah to abandon her here? Did she know? Was this all resentment over the transgressions against The Game that had deprived her of a pimp? Olivia was starting to get paranoid. Perhaps something was happening outside. Perhaps The Morality Front was daring another attack. Perhaps Sister Cecilia had simply forgotten she had left her here. It had been a long time since she had seen her, so there was no reason to assume she would remember her at all. Cecilia had a lot of novices to deal with.

When the paranoia had grown to its zenith and Olivia had decided that Ka'ssen and Cecilia had plotted her downfall psychically implanting the idea of executing the Vienna Job and conspired with The Pimp Council to go off and become lovers, Olivia found herself no longer alone. The company of other beings was a relief, although the other beings in question were not Sister Cecilia and this caused Olivia some trepidation.

There were four nuns, each wearing a different animal mask. One was a stag, another a bull, another a frog and the last a goat. The stag was tall and lean, her face framed by seagreen hair. The frog was shorter, broader big boned, her hands, the only skin her leather habit showed, were a burgundy color. The bull was clearly at least half cybernetic, her body making a quiet sloughing pounding noise like that of a microfiche. The goat, the only one not wearing the typical high leather boots of the order, stood on actual hooves, her arms, bared through a short sleeved habit were heavily knotted with muscle. She frightened him, yet at the same time or because she frightened him, she fascinated him. The goat held a thick leather whip.

The frog and the stag walked up to her. Viola swallowed hard. She did not know much of Geburah's training techniques, but that its sisters were ruthless and skilled at combining pain and pleasure, beauty and suffering, services she had once sold but he did not understand all that well. She stayed completely still, allowing the frog and the stag the opportunity to get close. Their movements were almost as robotic as the bull's as they pulled the white gown from her body. Seemingly from thin air, the bull produced a full length mirror, allowing Viola the first chance to glimpse her face and her body.

Green eyes. Long blonde hair. Small rounded nose. Plump lips. High, firm breasts with pale pink nipples. A flat stomach. Strong thighs. A cleanshaven thin-lipped vagina. She was beautiful enough to have warranted all of this attention. She missed the brightness of the orgone, the cock that was not a cock, but she did not truly feel this body lacked anything that it needed. She was the sort of ho that he would be proud to pander. After the initial glance she felt self-conscious, moving to cover up her breasts and sex.

As she did, the whip cracked behind her, smashing supersonic at her back. The goat wordlessly whipped her a second time, until she understood to uncross her arms and leave herself properly exposed. The frog took Viola's left nipple in her red hand, gently teasing it. The stag did the same with the right one, squeezing much harder, twisting and punishing.

"Oh!" she cried. The bull angrily shook her head. And behind her, the goat brought the whip down twice on her compact but rounded buttocks. She felt a cut open, streaking blood across the cheeks. The frog and stag switched tempos, good cop becoming bad, bad cop becoming good. The goat tenderly rubbed the open wound she had just created. Naked, vulnerable and scared, Viola was nonetheless enjoying these particular attentions, trying to exile from her mind the delightful thought of Sister Cecilia enacting these old beautiful rituals.

The goat surprised Viola with a swift hard spanking on her bloodstained ass. And a second, a third, a series of smaller more discreet strikes which began to feel nice, the pleasure in some of her body marrying itself to the pain in other parts of her. Though the touch of Dracula's brides, fanged and clawed and cruel had sometimes made her aware of the newness between her legs and caused it to boil, she felt a more pleasurable variation of this sensation under the pinching and the whip and the sight of her new female body, the body she had been sentenced to and feared getting to know. As the torture continued, she reflected upon how many times she had seen all women treated as if they had been sentenced thusly and as if a woman's body was itself a punishment.

How could something so pleasing be punishment? So pleasing as womanhood and so pleasing as the sublime beatings of the nuns of Geburah. As the heat grew inside she found herself wishing the nuns would touch her there. And she found herself allowing the words to pass her lips.

"Touch me," she begged, "please."

The stag's backhand was not as strong as her father's or as strong as Sister Cecilia's, so she did not fall back when she took the hit, in fact, as a former pimp, she took the slap to the face exquisitely. Her features remained serene but intense, eager to receive more pleasure and more violence. The stag backed away. The frog let go of her breast. The bull covered the mirror with a cloth. The goat ceased the rubbing and whipping alike. As soon as they arrived, they vanished. This reminded her of the brides of the count but not nearly so awful.

She laid down on the slab, body humming and burning, waiting, waiting again. For the first time since her transformation, she placed fingers inside herself and explored. And she was pleased with what her hands discovered on their journey. In the quiet of the cell, lying upon a stone slab and covered in marks and blood and welts on her back and buttocks, she experienced her first orgasm as a woman. The energy was new, more durable and more significant than the bursts of energy from his orgone. She eased into a timeless earthquake.

She resumed waiting. A few days spent in fantasy, meditation, masturbation, observation. She longed for the return of Cecilia and the four sisters but had no delusions of them arriving again soon, though oddly enough she had lost the fears of them never returning. She exercised, seeking to tighten and work her new muscles. The bodies of pimps were as they were, not needing exercise or much maintenance beyond the occasional gingerbread house, a pleasant shot of cognac or a burst of orgone. But this body sought improvement, being thoroughly human and conscious that it could be more perfect.

There was no monotony, but instead the development of an inner life that she had not thought possible. The lives of pimps were lives of stimulation and instant gratification, not of suffering of contemplation and to a certain extent not of determination. The Game was competitive to be sure and made pimps ambitious but playing The Game was just what it was and that was playing The Game. Life at Geburah was not monotony or a part of The Game, though being a ho she was a part of it. It was strange that someone capable of wielding something like an orgone cane dealt with so few contradictions and did not often to seek to reconcile them or strive for complexity or simplicity from life. Could it be possible that it was no worse to be a ho than it was to be a pimp?

The ceiling began to drip something hot and sweet, something that smelled of chocolate. And this was because the ceiling was beginning to drip hot chocolate. The welts and bruises from the agonies the sisters put her through were beginning to heal, so the falling drops of chocolate upon them stung mightily. It was odd that something so sweet was causing so much pain. She moved about the room attempting to dodge the falling drops, but the drips of chocolate moved with her, the drip apparently irresistible and implacable, unwilling to let her live without experiencing burning and sugar.

She cried from the pain like a bitch. This was not a pain that pleased her or made her feel like touching herself. She could see no route from burning chocolate to orgasm. But she did decide that maybe she should lie down on the floor and open her mouth. If she was going to experience the burning, perhaps the sweetness would be worth it as well. And it was. The chocolate was rich, dark and made her synapses spring to life. A feeling of warmth and contentment paired itself with the burning and scalding all over her body and a feeling of lightness. As with the whipping, the feelings interbred like the atoms she called together during her pimp days. Alchemy.

This was the meaning and origin of the power she had once possessed and in her consciousness in the wake of the falling chocolate, she still possessed it. She transmuted burning into joy, scalding into sweet ecstasy. She lay on the floor as the hot droplets fell and she returned once more to understanding her body and its responses.

By the time the rain of hot chocolate stopped, she had experienced an intense all consuming orgasm and an additional appreciation for the harsh training that she was undergoing. She sat up, returned to the slab and meditated, thankful for the belly full of chocolate that she had received. She worked out, contemplated and enjoyed the quiet and solitude of her cell. She looked into the mirror that the bull had left behind and examined and got to know her new body, thinking of it less as her new body and more as her body.

After another couple days of this, the bull, stag, frog and goat reappeared. She did not resist this time, helping the bull stand up the mirror. She did not ask to be touched, she did not flinch under the crack of the goat's whip. She exalted and basked in the gift she was given, the message the hot chocolate drips had given her. She accepted the pain with grace and humility and kissed each of her assailants before they took their leave of her. She was happy to see them again and knew that she would once more and was happy that this would occur.

The hot chocolate returned and she drank her fill with gratitude and enthusiasm, melting into the floor, into orgasm and into the hot chocolate consciousness. Beautiful Geburah. Generous Geburah. Generous chocolate. Generous womanhood. Her body, wet with chocolate, glowing with sweetness and gratitude felt as if had always been hers and if it had not, it was her destiny to have it. In the quiet of the cell, she cried tears of joy. She would once have thought she was crying like a bitch, but this was not so. And in the quiet of her cell, she danced.

Soon, she began to feel exactly how long the days were. She began to know how long she danced, masturbated, worked out, asked questions. How long the hot chocolate fell and how often the sisters arrived to teach her pain. She knew what to expect and gave herself clear duties and boundaries. She smiled and cried often. She kissed and embraced her sisters upon seeing them and thought of them as her sisters and they too in their punishments, in the language of the whip and the backhand began to tell her that she was one of them.

There came a day when the goat handed her her whip and bent before her. She held it with a quaking hand, at first hitting too gently, almost missing her target, then growing overzealous and striking too hard. The frog took the whip from her and punished her with it, hitting harder than the goat had ever hit to assert what it was to be the one holding the whip and remind her of the damage that could be caused. She apologized to the goat, holding her and kissing her tenderly seeking her forgiveness.

"Yes," said the goat in a voice deep but sweet, "I forgive you. We will see you again soon."

They did see each other again soon and when they did, Viola was careful with the whip. She used it with measured kindness, listened to its rhythms and heard it speak of the love behind the pain it inflicted. She used the whip tenderly but firmly as Sister Cecilia had always done, as an instrument of warmth and liberation. The goat took much pleasure in it. The frog sat down and presented herself immediately afterward and Viola carefully meted out her strikes, giving the frog waves of pleasure. The stag came next and did the same. Then at last the bull, whose half cybernetic body was very pain resistant. Viola felt tempted to use excessive force but took the whipping slowly with discipline and tenderness and had no problem showing the bull the hurting and loving she required.

The sisters gratefully kissed Viola's bare feet, hugged her, kissed her on the cheek and gave her their heartfelt thanks. And a few days later, they did this again and she grew better, crueler, sweeter and happier and they spoke afterwards, not just words but full conversations, sharing their thoughts upon what had occurred, regaling her with stories of their homeworlds and the jobs they had performed. She knew them soon as both sisters and dear, dear friends.

She was happy in the end to see Sister Cecilia who led her from the cell to an underground hot springs where she bathed her, washing off the blood and the sweat and the chocolate that had accumulated in her time in the chamber.

"You've done very well, Viola," said Sister Cecilia, "you seem less frightened, less angry and a lot more assertive."

Her smile and her blue eyes filled Viola's heart with joy and eyes with tears. She was grateful to be at Geburah and to be one of the sisters of the convent. And grateful to be in the surprisingly serene company of Sister Cecilia, who did wonders on the treatment of her wounds.

"Thank you, Mother Superior."

Cecilia kissed Viola's forehead.

"That is my title, but I am your sister always and a sister to all the sisters. Your sisters have shown me their marks and it is clear that you have developed an understanding of pain and pleasure and you have learned the lessons I brought from Netzach and from my dear friend from Earth."

It had not yet occurred to Viola the influence that visits to Netzach may have had on the running of Geburah. Geburah might once have been a place of more rigid discipline and harder cruelty before Cecilia joined Time Pimp's stable and traveled the universe administering pain for pleasure. Viola took pride in the accomplishments of Time Pimp, not believing them to be the work of a superior self, but of an equal but different one, one with a different agenda than she had.

"Your friend?" Viola asked.

"Yes," said Sister Cecilia, "he was the most famous man on Earth. He might have been the son of God, but it didn't matter if he was or not. What mattered was that he used the arts of love and alchemy to teach and that he taught me about suffering. Lessons that help me run this convent to this day."

When Viola was Time Pimp, she had felt that Cecilia's friend was an ungrateful Hater, one who appropriated the alchemy his shoes had compelled him to teach the long-haired skinnyass lame and used it to become famous and loved and to get ahead in The Game, while history knew him as the Hater, the most hated of history's Haters. She had grown jealous of the effect this man had on Sister Cecilia and the serenity he had given her, a serenity he felt had made the glorious rescue he had once done for her seem trivial.

"He told me the secret of dealing with clients and pimps. The secret was that you have to try to love everyone, but to know that love is an awful idea and is the same as all of the suffering you experience. The two meet in the same place and raise each other to the glory of life itself. And if you can't deal with that, then you're flat-out fucked. Because there's no alternative."

Viola thought of her envy once again and of how she had feared Sylvia. She thought of the pimpish provisions against giving up the cock or loving too deeply, even though they had come from a place that was the root of love and knew the workings of alchemy, the science of transformation which was the science of death which was in turn the science of love. She began to love the man who had caused scorn to be heaped on her adopted name for all eternity. She had thought the notoriety and accomplishment from The Vienna Job would undo the infamy her secret self had gotten from the Gethsemane Job. And it had, in an odd circuitous way succeeded. The Game was more vast, beautiful and complex than any pimp had ever known, The Game was love itself and pimps had always played it wrong.

"I love you, sister," said Viola, the words foreign but simple. They were not the words of a pimp or a ho, they were the words of a sister, a lover, a friend, a person. They surprised and brought her great joy.

"You mustn't say such things." The chill in Sister Cecilia's icy blue eyes filled the room. Absence, abuse and fear filled the room. And what happened next, the horror that fell upon Geburah, felt almost as if it had been invited by the sudden overflow of love. Whether it was that the words and thoughts had been so hard won that they could only have been born of agony or whether the outpouring was so sincere that That-Which-Wasn't-Love had to step in, it was uncertain, but time wombs opened and from them came forth the stench of decay and loathing and from them came forth the soldiers of repression and from them came forth the return to the dark and impossible.

Before the man she knew this heralded could show his face, Sister Cecilia had to make a quick decision and there was only one she could make. She drew her cutlass, mumbling words of hope, reassurance and sanctity and she removed her PTSD.

"Take this," she told Viola, "and run. Run through time until you find the man called Time Pimp. He's out there and he will save us."

Viola took the time travel device and set out on her journey. Whether accurate or not, Sister Cecilia's words simply had to be correct.

*The Hot Tub of Justice*

Viola had been preparing in her head an impassioned speech for pimpkind to assist Geburah. Perhaps even for her return to pimp stature, which seemed in the wake of Death Pimp's arrival, would be necessary. Viola had been preparing to stand up for herself and her identity and to stand up for Sister Cecilia's welfare. But Viola had not been prepared to arrive at The Hot Tub of Justice and find it vacant. There was only thing that could have happened and only one way it could have.

She panicked. She soaked awhile in the hot tub weeping like a bitch for the ones who had hurt her and the ones who had regulated The Game. What did it mean for them to be gone? Would The Game carry on or had it ended, won in one fell swoop by the force of Hate? She had fucked up. She had fucked up bad. She held her breath and descended to the bottom of the hot tub, closing her eyes and taking in all of the nothingness and no tomorrows around her.

"Time Pimp," said a familiar voice.

She did not initially know she was being spoken to, although the voice echoed through the chambers of her own head. Julius Baker. Her father was speaking to her. She emerged from the water, startled and relieved. She was even more startled and relieved to see that the clothes that Time

Pimp had left behind remained by the side of the tub as if waiting for her. Including the orgone cane and the platform shoes in which her father and uncle floated.

"Father?" she asked telepathically.

"Yes, my daughter. Put me on."

"I can't," she replied, "those are for pimps."

"Viola, you are a pimp and you will always be a pimp."

Hesitantly, she put on the purple velvet suit and the pimp hat. She could not see herself, but she knew that she looked good and right in this outfit. With this in mind giving her courage and certainty, she went even further, sliding her long, elegant feminine feet into the platform shoes, which molded themselves to her proportions, welcoming her back into them and back into the role she once played.

"Now," said Julius Baker, "you're going to have to defeat Death Pimp. But you're going to have to learn how to use the power you used to have, which is going to work differently in your new body."

"Ain't got time for that," Viola argued.

"There are places," said the other shoe, Time Pimp's Hater uncle, "where you have all the time in the world."

*Anhedonia*

In a city "protected" by a great dome of latex and an atmosphere of dark orgone, death, trauma and misplaced urges, in a convent once home to a noble order of lovely ladies that sought the best for those who came to them, in a throne room where latex covered sisters did nothing but listen to the doctrine of righteous necrophila in their brainwashed heads, Grand Etharch Pope Death Pimp was watching his mother and father fucking. Julius Baker was still very much alive, while Ka'ssen was clearly dead, her face no longer full of cunning and seduction but instead the blank subservience of a corpse brought to life by Death Pimp's black orgone. Several of his clients had approached him with offers for the dead Ka'ssen, but he had decided that it was more entertaining to watch his father replicate the act that had given him life. It was like being born again, which was the opposite of dying, which he never wanted to do. While Death Pimp gained succor from this, it went without saying that his father did not.

Julius was trying his hardest not to cry like a bitch, but he was not doing well at it. His orgone was flaccid, his energies constantly waning, almost turning black and deathly. He knew that if he could not get the energy up, that he risked Perpetual Torment or Perpetual Annihilation. Although Perpetual Torment could be little worse than being forced to fuck the dead woman with whom he had conceived his children for the entertainment of his least favorite of said children, one that he would kill if he had the chance, but since he could not kill him, he had no choice but to continuously work himself up to penetrate the lifeless Ka'ssen, her head-vagina no longer a place where bliss could be found but now just a dead, dry, receptive orifice caked with brain.

Death Pimp channeled blackness into his staff, forging it into a blade and slicing into the neck of his reanimated mother, who was beginning to bore him. It was a swift, sharp cut, decisive and capable. And it was good enough to send the head bouncing to the floor and once again make the lifeless body of Kjennen Ka'ssen slump over dead. Death Pimp toyed with the darkness and hate between his legs, spattering sparks of necrocum on his dead mother's blue body, causing it to twitch and move ineffectually, deprived of context by its severed head. The dark orgone faded again, almost nonexistent, leaving Death Pimp soft, empty, mad and scared.

"SEW IT BACK ON!" he screamed at one of the latexed attendants of the throne. The morality front slave moved quickly and capably, heating the latex of the battlesuit into a thick glue which fused Ka'ssen's head back into place. Death Pimp's hyperventilating ceased and he channeled a bolt of orgone through his staff, causing the dead Ka'ssen to spring to life again.

The attendant felt something odd. She felt like a she. She felt an awareness of possessing beautiful blue eyes and a soft, luxuriant foxcoat of red hair. She felt a memory of having happy, warm sensations and bringing happy, warm sensations.

She felt the memory of a man in purple velvet on shoes full of green liquor with creatures floating in them. This was not Death Pimp. This was not desire for the dead and annihilation. Something was wrong.

Feeling a tinge of panic, she reached into her brainwashing imagebank and found the pink-eyed angry, disapproving face of the Grand Etharch, the one universal truth, the creator and destroyer of all things. She remembered the Grand Etharch's words. "All memories outside of the cocoon of Our Lady of Perpetual Latex are lies trying to keep you from attaining oneness with the Grand Etharch." She did not want to be forbidden oneness with the Grand Etharch. That would be unthinkable. In her mind, she unmade the blue eyes, unmade the red hair, unmade the high perfect breasts and powerful legs. Unmade the things she had done outside the armor. It thanked the Grand Etharch for creating The Grand Etharch, who was really the only thing of consequence.

*The Time Womb*

Time Pimp who was Viola had gone to the one safe timeless place. Death Pimp would find her at The Time Casino and nowhere else would she be able to learn and perfect what she needed to learn. A ho dressed as a pimp, she felt foolish and her attempts to properly work the orgone cane more than confirmed it. She felt between her legs, projected outward, sought to explode around her. And it was just not working. The pimp fu techniques were fairly solid, the mass behind the backhand surprisingly intact, but alchemy and orgone generation were not quite there.

She was worried about this. Backhanding Death Pimp was liable to just put her within reach of the Perpetual Annihilation Device and that would be the end of it. She applied the meditations and techniques she had learned at Geburah, but was still not sure why the cane would not generate the spark that would fuck Death Pimp the fuck up or sex his drones to freedom. She was concerned.

"Your mother was a ho," the shoes were saying over and

over again, "and now you are a ho."

"I know!" she exclaimed, "I know. There's nothing to you more shameful than being a ho. Well, I was trained at the convent at Geburah. I am not ashamed to be a ho. I am a woman and women are powerful and women allow you to play The Game. You're no good without hos!"

That was when she figured out what Julius Baker had been getting at. She understood now what he meant about her mother being a ho and what he meant about her being a ho. It was not a cold, pimpish admonishment, but rather something completely and utterly different. He was explaining Ka'ssen and explaining Viola who was Time Pimp's heritage. There was a strength hidden in her blood and a power flowing through her body and it could be exploited.

Ka'ssen was the greatest of hos because her mind and her sex were one. And since the mind and sex were one, she was capable of becoming a place, a place of power, of beauty and of significance. She could draw those who made love her in and take them to euphoria. Since Ka'ssen had used this power only for deceit and malfeasance most of the time, Viola/Time Pimp did not understand what it meant or the ramifications of it.

But when she took the orgone cane in hand, calling out to sacred spaces, calling out the invitation and calling out receptivity, it came to life. She felt it gathering energy from around her, from the time womb and taking it in and understood the nature of this particular orgone. Instead of projecting out, she tried to move in and attract things from outside the time womb into it. Insects, small rodents and automotive parts flew about the air called inside by various worlds. And each insect and each rodent and each automotive part was in bliss.

Her mother was a ho and she while a pimp, was also a ho and there was no shame in being both and in fact, each being had man and woman, pimp and ho, dark and light orgone in them, each capable of receptive and projective principle. She practiced pimp fu and the alchemy of transformation in the time womb and got ready to go forth to Anhedonia to triumph.

*Anhedonia*

Sister Cecilia thought that she had known a man who helped her make money doing things that were not decent. She thought she thought that she had known of a world where the Grand Etharch was imperfect. She thought she had discovered that the Grand Etharch had an enemy. She thought she had thought she had fought next to this man, sword in hand claiming heads for love and liberty, when he had been reluctant to make his stand, afraid to really suffer and see suffering. She thought she had thought she had lain beside a thin, bearded man with the weight of worlds on his face and he had taught her things and she had taught him things. She thought she had thought she knew what it was to be a woman and she had taken great joy in it, even though she still fought through great sorrows and still lived in the hell that she was in now believing that it had been hell and not all there was. But she had only she thought these things. She did not think them.

Until she saw the blonde emerge from the open timewomb, wielding a rabbitheaded cane, dressed all in velvet, six feet high in absinthe filled platforms that reached out, whispering "yes, yes, yes, you are this" as the face of the Grand Etharch in her brainwashed mind said "no no no no." The rabbitheaded cane glowed with circles of orgone, telling her in her numbed latexed heart and soul "come to me, emerge, emerge, be born." The latex shook, resisted, hated. The armor, alive and dead as dead can be all at once had been made to resist the act of birth and realization. It spat the hot latex bullets it used to suppress nonbelievers, trying its best to strike the pimpclothed blonde and put an end to the cane's call to freedom, the cane's birth energies.

The bullets came out scattered and when they did not, the womb circles around the cane became a forcefield, attracting and then repulsing them. The expressionless facial muscles of the veritable bodybag in which Sister Cecilia was enclosed contorted, its mouth opened, giving her own mouth a chance to breathe and to part its pomegranate lips.

"Time Pimp?"

She struggled for the use of her hands, which wanted only to make bullets or to choke the intruder to death. She peeled the latex from the fingers of her other hand, exposing a hand, defiantly baring the flesh that was expressly forbidden in Death Pimp's world.

"Is that you? I'm stuck in here."

"You aren't," said Time Pimp, charging the cane with tenderness and compassion, with the force that brought life into being. The pink concentric circles surrounded Sister Cecilia, who was peeling the latex off her other hand.

Death Pimp had been watching this spectacle aghast. How was a mere ho wielding the orgone cane? How could a ho have the inner strength to liberate herself from the latex?

"How are you doing this? Who are you?"

"I'm Time Pimp," said Time Pimp, "you jiveass motherfucker."

Death Pimp lashed out with a tentacle of dark orgone, an angry burst of unmaking from his staff. Time Pimp countered the attack by calling forth another tunnel of circles, pink light appearing in the air in front of the dark orgone burst, encompassing it, squeezing it, rendering it smaller and smaller until the darkness spent itself and disappeared.

Death Pimp showed a good deal of annoyance at this. He brought his staff down hard on the tortured Julius Baker's head.

"You planned this! You made him to be a pimp and a ho!"

Death Pimp desperately banged the staff on the floor, summoning a yellowed emaciated Professor Panda.

"Get him PAID!" The Grand Etharch declared.

Wordlessly, weakly, soullessly and without protest, the filthy longlost panda hit the button on his remote that opened the PAID's eye, bringing forth its life-destroying appendages. Time Pimp breathed deeply. Perpetual Annihilation. The great unknowable and undoable. The thing he had always feared Death Pimp would get his hands on. She had done much to resist this thing, standing up to Death Pimp the once but otherwise making no attempt to put an end to his Hater's hate.

She trusted her body. She trusted the orgone cane, she

trusted. Alone in the timewomb she had relearned orgone crafting, relearned alchemy as the craft of trust. When reassured that it can be something better, the atom will trust its mate and they will give birth to substances compounds, elements, oils, philters, ferris wheels and forest fires. The pink spirals of time womb expanded around her, seeking to take in more, inviting the death machine to get itself lost.

Bearing all its tentacles down upon a single point, shedding a tear from its single robotic eye, the Perpetual Annihilation and Impurification Device became curious, eager, ambitious and happy, seeking to annihilate but to explore, putting an end to Perpetual Annihilation, a Perpetual End to Perpetual Annihilation, a doomsday weapon offering the gift of a gentle escape into night and possibility.

"Whore!" Death Pimp hissed, "You whore!"

An orgone powered time womb opened, drawing both Time Pimp and Death Pimp into it and the two disappeared.

*The Time Womb*

"I'll kill you, whore!" said Death Pimp for the ten-thousandth time, releasing for the ten thousandth time, a burst of dark orgone from his staff, that disappeared into the mysteries of the orgone cane's pink orgone shield. Death Pimp's hate ran almost infinitely deep, but he was growing weary of the struggles.

"Why must you?" asked Death Pimp, sitting down, holding his knees, "why must you stop me?"

Time Pimp was simply floored by the question. There seemed almost no reason to answer it. Had Death Pimp never been aware of the nature of the game? Julius Baker had drilled it into their heads almost from birth. But the orgone shield, smooth pink icy sparkling, an electric-sorbet suggested there be no attack, no judgment.

"You're a Hater.. You've got to hate."

"Yes," Death Pimp hissed, "I hate so much."

"Our father had a father," said Time Pimp, not quite understanding what he was saying, "and Ka'ssen had a mother.

Imagine Ka'ssen's mother."

Death Pimp sat imagining. He was caught up in the thought for what have been several minutes or several years. Since they were inside of a timewomb, it did not particularly matter. Unless it did. Nobody knew how time travel worked. Death Pimp had not in his years of hate, panic, and oppression given himself time to think about such things and this place felt nice, like he had always hoped the anuses and vaginas of the dead would feel and they never really did. He had secretly wondered what it was that made his clients buy the reanimated hos he pimped. But not for very long, since thinking got in the way of his hating.

"I don't want to die," he said soberly. This was the first time since their childhood together that Time Pimp had heard Death Pimp speaking calmly without shouting or propaganda or death threats or cackling.

"Nobody wants to die," said Time Pimp, "but everybody does."

"Not if I can kill you," said Death Pimp, "but you broke my Perpetual Annihilation and Impurification Device. So now I have to live, suffer and die."

"It's all in The Game, though. We live, we suffer, we die. Or we become shoes which is as close to dying as pimps come."

"I don't want to be shoes."

Time Pimp nodded. It seemed like the lives of the octopi in their shoes were dull, anticlimactic and sad. Except for the privilege of guiding pimps somewhere else, which Julius Baker had not done all that well. Julius both hated him doing the Vienna Job and wanted him to do it. He had treated his sons less than great and said it was all part of The Game and said that all that was important was getting paid. But PAID was ugly. PAID had annihilated the pimp council. They got PAID and lost The Game.

"We had a bad Playa and a bad Hater. And they made bad shoes."

Death Pimp pulled a flask from his robe, gathering time dew from the womb in it. He passed it to Time Pimp.

"Make it booze."

"Sounds like a good idea."

Time Pimp held the flask in his hand commanding the atoms of Time Dew to breed for generations, selecting the alchemical traits of a fine thousand-year-old Scotch. It was sweeter, sharper more intense than the cognac she had made during her pimp days. And the two drank together and they got drunk. For some time, they sat like that together inside the Time Womb, quiet and drunk and not thinking about things like Perpetual Annihilation.

"Hey," said Time Pimp, "I think I know what we gotta do. Do you trust me?"

*Netzach*

Licorice heat. Agua Florida. Temporal Dew and nude luminescence. Ten thousand ebony saxophones on the streets of the city outside whose borders they had landed. On a rocky emerald outcropping above a hot pale green waterfall that smelled not just like anise but like the word itself, like the idea of anise. As much anise as something could be. As the absinthe cascaded down into the absinthe sea, fumes and spray rose up into the brother and sister's noses, tickling them and opening their consciousnesses to wormwood salvation.

Death Pimp staggered, wobbled. Shook his head and grew intense. He charged the black up on his staff, though it came slowly and took all of his resources, all of his concentration to make the little snake of black that bounced off the time radiation around his sister.

"YOU CUNT! You tricked me!"

He lunged. She dodged, tripped him, made him tumble down, a sharp emerald spike opening a gash in the back of his head. His mitre tumbled off, which drove him into a deeper rage. Though dazed and drunk, bleeding from the back of his skull, he came at her hard, swinging the staff and shattering several of her ribs. Though holding her injured ribcage with one hand, she still managed to emit a burst of pink light from the orgone cane that pulled Death Pimp closer, the force of its traction unbalancing him and loosening his grip on the staff. Though hurt, Time Pimp knew she wouldn't have many chances. Death Pimp was within reach and she was pulsing with pink orgone. She had to reach him somehow. She did not kick, did not headbutt or use her nun's training to plan the perfect caning. She grabbed him. And she held him. Though her ribs were in pain, though this man had once again affirmed he was her enemy, she held him.

"Don't struggle," she said, "you are my brother and I love you."

"I hate you. You've tricked me!"

"I haven't."

"I don't want to do this but I want to do this."

Time Pimp wanted to do this but did not want to do this. Death smelled like wormwood and anise. Death smelled like possibility and change and hope that the future would be something else. Yet death was death. Death was the end of Time Pimp and an end to The Game. It was Death Pimp's long suffering and secret exuberance that spurred her onward and let her know this had to be done. Time Pimp fought not to grieve for life and the people she would never see again, Sylvia, Sister Cecilia, Sherlock Holmes, even Professor Panda. They would be grieving for her, they would be hurt, but the hurt was a force of love, a force for love.

"Take a step back," said Time Pimp, eyes locked in her brother's.

Death Pimp took a step back. His sister did not let go nor did she break from his gaze. Though her ribs were broken, she was squeezing him hard.

"We're going to turn into wisdom and into love. There will be a pimp who will wear us and he will know what we know and he will play The Game wisely. That's the most you need to know."

The pink orgone wrapped around them, but did not transport them. It brought them comfort and relief, it shocked them for a moment by the revealing the depths of their pain and terror, but when it stopped, the both of them knew it was the same force that made this happen. Death Pimp and Time

Pimp backed up to the very edge, still embraced.

"You make a good-looking whore," said Death Pimp.

Time Pimp nodded solemnly and smiling a big, feminine smile she pushed against Death Pimp. Death Pimp let her, even as he knew there was no more cliff and what lie below was an eternity as something that was neither pimp nor Hater and an end to consciousness as they understood it. The smell of anise, wormwood and alcohol in their noses, they breathed deep, knowing it was the last breath they would ever take and that what was below was all they would ever taste for all eternity.

They fell. At last landing with a splash into the absinthe sea of Netzach, into an eternity inside of a pair of shoes.

*Geburah, one year later*

Mother Cecilia liked to witness the executions. They reminded her that cruel as the universe, cruel as time, cruel as history were, they would always be both loving and just. As the girls kissed, massaged and forgave criminals into redemption, her heart often heavy floated, not quite taking off but lighting itself on a sea of It's Alright, bobbing, treading, debating whether it would sink or it would reach the shores of acceptance. She did not know what it was that Time Pimp had done, but she had breathed again and she had accepted the title she deserved though never used gratefully.

Watching a warthogheaded, crab-bodied alien get his just desserts was not doing it today, however. Nor was seeing him soothed and heading toward betterness and joy. In losing Time Pimp, she had lost both Time Pimp and Viola and she cared a lot for them. Today was her birthday, a concept that mattered neither on Anhedonia or Geburah, but once somebody had cared about it and done something with her. She had taught the secrets of pain and grief and love and how they were one but she had difficulty believing the tenets of her faith today, whether or not Jesus Christ himself had spoken to her of them.

She should have been more surprised when she saw the Purple Cadillac parked on the street. She should have been more surprised that her bronzed, gaudy platform shoe'd employer stepped out of it. After all, nobody understood time travel.

"Happy birthday, Mother Superior," he said, "why don't you get in the car?"

*Epilogue:*
*The Looking Glass Paradox*
*1890, England*

It was brilliant, shiny black, the juggernaut, dragon-winged, remorafaced. Swaying round on awkward, stilty legs, gnashing bioorganic teeth, lashing out with claws to get hold of Time Pimp and Cecilia. Cecilia with her expertise in swordsmanship had littered the ground with many of the drill-nosed green pigs that the pandas and lionheads had sent as advance scouts. It was getting close and though the puddle of alchemized mercury had slowed it down, it had not stopped the juggernaut altogether. That was up to the Reverend Charles Lutwidge Dodgson, inputting a series of digits to work a jury-rigged orgone powered Difference Beam pointed up at the great robotic bird overhead in whose chest lay the control crystal for the juggernaut.

Time Pimp's orgone cane had been charged up and was being used to run the Difference Beam. So, he was quite unarmed in the face of the panda/lionhead juggernaut. While unsure if it had the capacity to outright kill him, Time Pimp did know that the juggernaut could spend a very long time digesting him and there was no telling what the two most loathsome races in history would put inside of such a thing.

So, it was a relief when the Difference Beam shot out a series of glowing digits, flying upward, smacking into the bird's control crystal, bouncing down and with enhanced speed and intensity, slicing into the juggernaut's neck, severing its head. The stilty-legs wobbled, the body fell. The panda scout ships in the sky exploded all at once. The giant drillpenises of lionhead mining spiders went flaccid before even breaking the surface. There was an eerie calm, a correctness that made everyone uncomfortable. Time Pimp shivered a little, the invisible hand of "it never ends" smearing his face in excrement. But he took a deep breath as the invasion fell apart. Because it never ends.

Professor Panda emerged from a makeshift medical tent, carrying a jar of silicate locusts. Had the poor Victorians at Piccadilly Circus not just been subjected to sexual humiliation and forced breeding by the lionheads, this would have been a confusing sight for them.

"Looks like we're in the clear. I've extracted the nanovirus and I will take my leave to return Elvis to his own time."

"Nice work, Professor," replied Time Pimp, giving the panda a genuinely kind pat on the head.

Professor Panda extended a paw to the Reverend Dodgson. "It was a pleasure to meet you, sir. You are a great man."

The awkward, droopy faced young academician smiled vaguely without making eye contact.

"Pleasure to meet you as well. You're quite the scientist."

"Well, I must go," said Professor Panda, turning toward the tent, "he needs to get home soon. He's all shook up."

Nobody laughed. Elvis had actually been quite traumatized. It would take weeks of compulsive overeating for him to recover emotionally from what he had just endured as a slave to the pandas. So, Professor Panda was quick to return to the king and take him back to the 1950s where he belonged.

It was then that Sherlock Holmes and Watson came running breathlessly, Watson carrying a hogtied Kjennen Ka'ssen, which he placed at Sister Cecilia. Holmes approached the Reverend Dodgson.

"I'd like to thank you," he said, "your expertise in mathematics was instrumental in breaking those codes. Moriarty remains at large, but at least Kjennen Ka'ssen has been recaptured and Queen Victoria has been freed from a lifetime of erotic servitude."

"Yes, well, that's umm…that's…" the Reverend stammered, "that's certainly better than the alternative, isn't it?"

"It's a shame that as Victorians we will have to ignore this forever and you won't be declared a national hero, but we will have deep gratitude in our hearts," said Holmes.

"Yes, societal repression and all that."

"I'm so glad you understand. Her Majesty was concerned that you'd…"

"No, no, I'm fine with it."

Time Pimp came up from behind the Reverend, clapping him on the shoulder.

"Nice work. You look like you could use a breath of fresh air. Let's go get some air."

They got into the purple Cadillac and they drove through time and space until Time Pimp found the freshest air he knew.

*Netzach*

The Reverend Charles Dodgson, surprised and elated, sat beside Time Pimp in the petals of a mile high orchid that provided a wonderful view of much of Netzach and an excellent view of the shining nude sun. The air was thick with opium, girl and Agua Florida, sweet, sexy and honest, pleasing to the eye, seductive to the nose, full of music and tickling his being beneath his clothes. Saxophones, dancing prostitutes, buildings made of flowers and light of a seductive sun were so unlike the world he had just seen in the hands of the lionheads and the one before they came that also displeased him so.

"I think," said the Reverend, "that this is the only place that makes any sense at all."

"I would agree to that."

Flocks of stained glass doves circled them overhead. The Reverend tossed his head back and laughed and laughed and laughed until he wept. He had told the truth and there were no places outside of this one that made even half as much sense as it did. He was going to return to a world where bureaucracy and hypocrisy and classism and a labyrinth of manners cut people off from almost everything that this place meant. And there was a little girl who he treasured with all his timid heart who would grow up in that place, be encompassed by it and live in its lies and confusions and its lack of stained glass doves and dancing saxophones. He felt angry that he had just saved such a world. The alternative might have been worse but at its best it still made no damn sense. He could not save the girl from the world that he had saved.

"Why did I bother?"

Time Pimp shrugged.

"What else were you gonna do? Let it die."

"Suppose not, but I still don't like it."

Time Pimp handed the Reverend a glass of cognac.

"Drink."

"I don't really…"

"Just drink."

They silently toasted to Agua Florida and absinthe and stained glass doves and buildings made of flowers and saxophone parades. The two men drank and drank again and drank again, until they were almost on the brink of passing out inside of a giant orchid.

"You've seen the future," said the Reverend, "can you tell me something?"

Time Pimp didn't know if he could. But he would.

"Sure."

"I don't think it will work out with Alice," said the Reverend, letting the halfborn question float.

"I don't think it will either. But you're going to write something and give her a great gift. It won't just be a gift for her either."

"Well, that's good."

The Reverend took another drink.

"So, is it just going to hurt me? Is it going to turn out badly. Is she going to get old and move on and forget about me?"

"I'm going to say yes."

"So why should I bother?"

Time Pimp shrugged.

"What else are you gonna do? It's a terrible idea, but there's nothing else."

Eyes wet, his awkward face sad, the man who would be Lewis Carroll looked earnestly at his time traveling pimp friend.

"So what are you saying I should do."

"I don't know. Just tell a good story I guess."

*1890, the English countryside*

It was a sunny day and the Reverend Charles Dodgson was rowing two little girls in a boat. They listened with rapt attention as he began to tell them a story. The youngest, Alice was particularly entranced, as it was a story about her. The story was about sense and nonsense, about the perilous world they would grow up in and the need to keep a good head one's shoulders as one traversed it. To those who weren't listening, it would have seemed like a simple fairy tale or at best a masterwork of nonsense, but that was not so.

It was, like all the best stories, the ones really worth telling, a love story.

## ABOUT THE AUTHOR

**GARRETT COOK** is a writer, editor and a businessman. His books include the *Murderland* series, *Archelon Ranch*, *Jimmy Plush, Teddy Bear Detective* and the *Satan's Mummy* series (as Henry Price). He is the editor of *Imperial Youth Review*. And if you listen to everything he tells you, you just might get out of this alive.

# BIZARRO BOOKS

## CATALOG    SPRING 2013

**ERASERHEAD PRESS**

Your major resource for the bizarro fiction genre:

# WWW.BIZARROCENTRAL.COM

Introduce yourselves to the bizarro fiction genre and all of its authors with the Bizarro Starter Kit series. Each volume features short novels and short stories by ten of the leading bizarro authors, designed to give you a perfect sampling of the genre for only $10.

## BB-0X1
### "The Bizarro Starter Kit" (Orange)
Featuring D. Harlan Wilson, Carlton Mellick III, Jeremy Robert Johnson, Kevin L Donihe, Gina Ranalli, Andre Duza, Vincent W. Sakowski, Steve Beard, John Edward Lawson, and Bruce Taylor. **236 pages   $10**

## BB-0X2
### "The Bizarro Starter Kit" (Blue)
Featuring Ray Fracalossy, Jeremy C. Shipp, Jordan Krall, Mykle Hansen, Andersen Prunty, Eckhard Gerdes, Bradley Sands, Steve Aylett, Christian TeBordo, and Tony Rauch. **244 pages   $10**

## BB-0X2
### "The Bizarro Starter Kit" (Purple)
Featuring Russell Edson, Athena Villaverde, David Agranoff, Matthew Revert, Andrew Goldfarb, Jeff Burk, Garrett Cook, Kris Saknussemm, Cody Goodfellow, and Cameron Pierce **264 pages $10**

BB-001 "The Kafka Effekt" D. Harlan Wilson — A collection of forty-four irreal short stories loosely written in the vein of Franz Kafka, with more than a pinch of William S. Burroughs sprinkled on top. **211 pages** **$14**

BB-002 "Satan Burger" Carlton Mellick III — The cult novel that put Carlton Mellick III on the map ... Six punks get jobs at a fast food restaurant owned by the devil in a city violently overpopulated by surreal alien cultures. **236 pages** **$14**

BB-003 "Some Things Are Better Left Unplugged" Vincent Sakwoski — Join The Man and his Nemesis, the obese tabby, for a nightmare roller coaster ride into this postmodern fantasy. **152 pages** **$10**

BB-005 "Razor Wire Pubic Hair" Carlton Mellick III — A genderless humandildo is purchased by a razor dominatrix and brought into her nightmarish world of bizarre sex and mutilation. **176 pages** **$11**

BB-007 "The Baby Jesus Butt Plug" Carlton Mellick III — Using clones of the Baby Jesus for anal sex will be the hip sex fetish of the future. **92 pages** **$10**

BB-010 "The Menstruating Mall" Carlton Mellick III — "The Breakfast Club meets Chopping Mall as directed by David Lynch." - Brian Keene **212 pages** **$12**

BB-011 "Angel Dust Apocalypse" Jeremy Robert Johnson — Meth-heads, man-made monsters, and murderous Neo-Nazis. "Seriously amazing short stories..." - Chuck Palahniuk, author of Fight Club **184 pages** **$11**

BB-015 "Foop!" Chris Genoa — Strange happenings are going on at Dactyl, Inc, the world's first and only time travel tourism company.
"A surreal pie in the face!" - Christopher Moore **300 pages** **$14**

BB-032 **"Extinction Journals" Jeremy Robert Johnson** — An uncanny voyage across a newly nuclear America where one man must confront the problems associated with loneliness, insane dieties, radiation, love, and an ever-evolving cockroach suit with a mind of its own. **104 pages $10**

BB-037 **"The Haunted Vagina" Carlton Mellick III** — It's difficult to love a woman whose vagina is a gateway to the world of the dead. **132 pages $10**

BB-043 **"War Slut" Carlton Mellick III** — Part "1984," part "Waiting for Godot," and part action horror video game adaptation of John Carpenter's "The Thing." **116 pages $10**

BB-047 **"Sausagey Santa" Carlton Mellick III** — A bizarro Christmas tale featuring Santa as a piratey mutant with a body made of sausages. 124 pages $10

BB-048 **"Misadventures in a Thumbnail Universe" Vincent Sakowski** — Dive deep into the surreal and satirical realms of neo-classical Blender Fiction, filled with television shoes and flesh-filled skies. **120 pages $10**

BB-053 **"Ballad of a Slow Poisoner" Andrew Goldfarb** — Millford Mutterwurst sat down on a Tuesday to take his afternoon tea, and made the unpleasant discovery that his elbows were becoming flatter. **128 pages $10**

BB-055 **"Help! A Bear is Eating Me" Mykle Hansen** — The bizarro, heartwarming, magical tale of poor planning, hubris and severe blood loss...
**150 pages $11**

BB-056 **"Piecemeal June" Jordan Krall** — A man falls in love with a living sex doll, but with love comes danger when her creator comes after her with crab-squid assassins. **90 pages $9**

BB-058 **"The Overwhelming Urge" Andersen Prunty** — A collection of bizarro tales by Andersen Prunty. **150 pages  $11**

BB-059 **"Adolf in Wonderland" Carlton Mellick III** — A dreamlike adventure that takes a young descendant of Adolf Hitler's design and sends him down the rabbit hole into a world of imperfection and disorder. **180 pages  $11**

BB-061 **"Ultra Fuckers" Carlton Mellick III** — Absurdist suburban horror about a couple who enter an upper middle class gated community but can't find their way out. **108 pages  $9**

BB-062 **"House of Houses" Kevin L. Donihe** — An odd man wants to marry his house. Unfortunately, all of the houses in the world collapse at the same time in the Great House Holocaust. Now he must travel to House Heaven to find his departed fiancee. **172 pages  $11**

BB-064 **"Squid Pulp Blues" Jordan Krall** — In these three bizarro-noir novellas, the reader is thrown into a world of murderers, drugs made from squid parts, deformed gun-toting veterans, and a mischievous apocalyptic donkey. **204 pages $12**

BB-065 **"Jack and Mr. Grin" Andersen Prunty** — "When Mr. Grin calls you can hear a smile in his voice. Not a warm and friendly smile, but the kind that seizes your spine in fear. You don't need to pay your phone bill to hear it. That smile is in every line of Prunty's prose." - Tom Bradley. **208 pages  $12**

BB-066 **"Cybernetrix" Carlton Mellick III** — What would you do if your normal everyday world was slowly mutating into the video game world from Tron? **212 pages $12**

BB-072 **"Zerostrata" Andersen Prunty** — Hansel Nothing lives in a tree house, suffers from memory loss, has a very eccentric family, and falls in love with a woman who runs naked through the woods every night. **144 pages $11**

BB-073 **"The Egg Man" Carlton Mellick III** — It is a world where humans reproduce like insects. Children are the property of corporations, and having an enormous ten-foot brain implanted into your skull is a grotesque sexual fetish. Mellick's industrial urban dystopia is one of his darkest and grittiest to date. **184 pages $11**

BB-074 **"Shark Hunting in Paradise Garden" Cameron Pierce** — A group of strange humanoid religious fanatics travel back in time to the Garden of Eden to discover it is invested with hundreds of giant flying maneating sharks. **150 pages $10**

BB-075 **"Apeshit" Carlton Mellick III** - Friday the 13th meets Visitor Q. Six hipster teens go to a cabin in the woods inhabited by a deformed killer. An incredibly fucked-up parody of B-horror movies with a bizarro slant. **192 pages $12**

BB-076 **"Fuckers of Everything on the Crazy Shitting Planet of the Vomit At smosphere" Mykle Hansen** - Three bizarro satires. Monster Cocks, Journey to the Center of Agnes Cuddlebottom, and Crazy Shitting Planet. **228 pages $12**

BB-077 **"The Kissing Bug" Daniel Scott Buck** — In the tradition of Roald Dahl, Tim Burton, and Edward Gorey, comes this bizarro anti-war children's story about a bohemian conenose kissing bug who falls in love with a human woman. **116 pages $10**

BB-078 **"MachoPoni" Lotus Rose** — It's My Little Pony... *Bizarro* style! A long time ago Poniworld was split in two. On one side of the Jagged Line is the Pastel Kingdom, a magical land of music, parties, and positivity. On the other side of the Jagged Line is Dark Kingdom inhabited by an army of undead ponies. **148 pages $11**

BB-079 **"The Faggiest Vampire" Carlton Mellick III** — A Roald Dahl-esque children's story about two faggy vampires who partake in a mustache competition to find out which one is truly the faggiest. **104 pages $10**

BB-080 **"Sky Tongues" Gina Ranalli** — The autobiography of Sky Tongues, the biracial hermaphrodite actress with tongues for fingers. Follow her strange life story as she rises from freak to fame. **204 pages $12**

**BB-081 "Washer Mouth" Kevin L. Donihe** - A washing machine becomes human and pursues his dream of meeting his favorite soap opera star. **244 pages $11**

**BB-082 "Shatnerquake" Jeff Burk** - All of the characters ever played by William Shatner are suddenly sucked into our world. Their mission: hunt down and destroy the real William Shatner. **100 pages $10**

**BB-083 "The Cannibals of Candyland" Carlton Mellick III** - There exists a race of cannibals that are made of candy. They live in an underground world made out of candy. One man has dedicated his life to killing them all. **170 pages $11**

**BB-084 "Slub Glub in the Weird World of the Weeping Willows" Andrew Goldfarb** - The charming tale of a blue glob named Slub Glub who helps the weeping willows whose tears are flooding the earth. There are also hyenas, ghosts, and a voodoo priest **100 pages $10**

**BB-085 "Super Fetus" Adam Pepper** - Try to abort this fetus and he'll kick your ass! **104 pages $10**

**BB-086 "Fistful of Feet" Jordan Krall** - A bizarro tribute to spaghetti westerns, featuring Cthulhu-worshipping Indians, a woman with four feet, a crazed gunman who is obsessed with sucking on candy, Syphilis-ridden mutants, sexually transmitted tattoos, and a house devoted to the freakiest fetishes. **228 pages $12**

**BB-087 "Ass Goblins of Auschwitz" Cameron Pierce** - It's Monty Python meets Nazi exploitation in a surreal nightmare as can only be imagined by Bizarro author Cameron Pierce. **104 pages $10**

**BB-088 "Silent Weapons for Quiet Wars" Cody Goodfellow** - "This is high-end psychological surrealist horror meets bottom-feeding low-life crime in a techno-thrilling science fiction world full of Lovecraft and magic..." -John Skipp **212 pages $12**

BB-089 **"Warrior Wolf Women of the Wasteland" Carlton Mellick III**
— Road Warrior Werewolves versus McDonaldland Mutants...post-apocalyptic fiction has never been quite like this. **316 pages $13**

BB-091 **"Super Giant Monster Time" Jeff Burk** — A tribute to choose your own adventures and Godzilla movies. Will you escape the giant monsters that are rampaging the fuck out of your city and shit? Or will you join the mob of alien-controlled punk rockers causing chaos in the streets? What happens next depends on you. **188 pages $12**

BB-092 **"Perfect Union" Cody Goodfellow** — "Cronenberg's THE FLY on a grand scale: human/insect gene-spliced body horror, where the human hive politics are as shocking as the gore." -John Skipp. **272 pages $13**

BB-093 **"Sunset with a Beard" Carlton Mellick III** — 14 stories of surreal science fiction. **200 pages $12**

BB-094 **"My Fake War" Andersen Prunty** — The absurd tale of an unlikely soldier forced to fight a war that, quite possibly, does not exist. It's Rambo meets Waiting for Godot in this subversive satire of American values and the scope of the human imagination. **128 pages $11**

BB-095 **"Lost in Cat Brain Land" Cameron Pierce** — Sad stories from a surreal world. A fascist mustache, the ghost of Franz Kafka, a desert inside a dead cat. Primordial entities mourn the death of their child. The desperate serve tea to mysterious creatures. A hopeless romantic falls in love with a pterodactyl. And much more. **152 pages $11**

BB-096 **"The Kobold Wizard's Dildo of Enlightenment +2" Carlton Mellick III** — A Dungeons and Dragons parody about a group of people who learn they are only made up characters in an AD&D campaign and must find a way to resist their nerdy teenaged players and retarded dungeon master in order to survive. 232 **pages $12**

BB-098 **"A Hundred Horrible Sorrows of Ogner Stump" Andrew Goldfarb** — Goldfarb's acclaimed comic series. A magical and weird journey into the horrors of everyday life. **164 pages $11**

BB-099 **"Pickled Apocalypse of Pancake Island" Cameron Pierce**—A demented fairy tale about a pickle, a pancake, and the apocalypse. **102 pages $8**

BB-100 **"Slag Attack" Andersen Prunty**— Slag Attack features four visceral, noir stories about the living, crawling apocalypse. A slag is what survivors are calling the slug-like maggots raining from the sky, burrowing inside people, and hollowing out their flesh and their sanity. **148 pages $11**

BB-101 **"Slaughterhouse High" Robert Devereaux**—A place where schools are built with secret passageways, rebellious teens get zippers installed in their mouths and genitals, and once a year, on that special night, one couple is slaughtered and the bits of their bodies are kept as souvenirs. **304 pages $13**

BB-102 **"The Emerald Burrito of Oz" John Skipp & Marc Levinthal**—OZ IS REAL! Magic is real! The gate is really in Kansas! And America is finally allowing Earth tourists to visit this weird-ass, mysterious land. But when Gene of Los Angeles heads off for summer vacation in the Emerald City, little does he know that a war is brewing...a war that could destroy both worlds. **280 pages $13**

BB-103 **"The Vegan Revolution... with Zombies" David Agranoff** — When there's no more meat in hell, the vegans will walk the earth. **160 pages $11**

BB-104 **"The Flappy Parts" Kevin L Donihe**—Poems about bunnies, LSD, and police abuse. You know, things that matter. 132 **pages $11**

BB-105 **"Sorry I Ruined Your Orgy" Bradley Sands**—Bizarro humorist Bradley Sands returns with one of the strangest, most hilarious collections of the year. **130 pages $11**

BB-106 **"Mr. Magic Realism" Bruce Taylor**—Like Golden Age science fiction comics written by Freud, *Mr. Magic Realism* is a strange, insightful adventure that spans the furthest reaches of the galaxy, exploring the hidden caverns in the hearts and minds of men, women, aliens, and biomechanical cats. **152 pages $11**

BB-107 **"Zombies and Shit" Carlton Mellick III**—"Battle Royale" meets "Return of the Living Dead." Mellick's bizarro tribute to the zombie genre. **308 pages $13**

BB-108 **"The Cannibal's Guide to Ethical Living" Mykle Hansen**— Over a five star French meal of fine wine, organic vegetables and human flesh, a lunatic delivers a witty, chilling, disturbingly sane argument in favor of eating the rich.. **184 pages $11**

BB-109 **"Starfish Girl" Athena Villaverde**—In a post-apocalyptic underwater dome society, a girl with a starfish growing from her head and an assassin with sea anenome hair are on the run from a gang of mutant fish men. **160 pages $11**

BB-110 **"Lick Your Neighbor" Chris Genoa**—Mutant ninjas, a talking whale, kung fu masters, maniacal pilgrims, and an alcoholic clown populate Chris Genoa's surreal, darkly comical and unnerving reimagining of the first Thanksgiving. **303 pages $13**

BB-111 **"Night of the Assholes" Kevin L. Donihe**—A plague of assholes is infecting the countryside. Normal everyday people are transforming into jerks, snobs, dicks, and douchebags. And they all have only one purpose: to make your life a living hell.. **192 pages $11**

BB-112 **"Jimmy Plush, Teddy Bear Detective" Garrett Cook**—Hardboiled cases of a private detective trapped within a teddy bear body. **180 pages $11**

BB-113 **"The Deadheart Shelters" Forrest Armstrong**—The hip hop lovechild of William Burroughs and Dali... **144 pages $11**

BB-114 **"Eyeballs Growing All Over Me... Again" Tony Raugh**— Absurd, surreal, playful, dream-like, whimsical, and a lot of fun to read. **144 pages $11**

BB-115 **"Whargoul" Dave Brockie** — From the killing grounds of Stalingrad to the death camps of the holocaust. From torture chambers in Iraq to race riots in the United States, the Whargoul was there, killing and raping. **244 pages $12**

BB-116 **"By the Time We Leave Here, We'll Be Friends" J. David Osborne** — A David Lynchian nightmare set in a Russian gulag, where its prisoners, guards, traitors, soldiers, lovers, and demons fight for survival and their own rapidly deteriorating humanity. **168 pages $11**

BB-117 **"Christmas on Crack" edited by Carlton Mellick III** — Perverted Christmas Tales for the whole family! . . . as long as every member of your family is over the age of 18. **168 pages $11**

BB-118 **"Crab Town" Carlton Mellick III** — Radiation fetishists, balloon people, mutant crabs, sail-bike road warriors, and a love affair between a woman and an H-Bomb. This is one mean asshole of a city. Welcome to Crab Town. **100 pages $8**

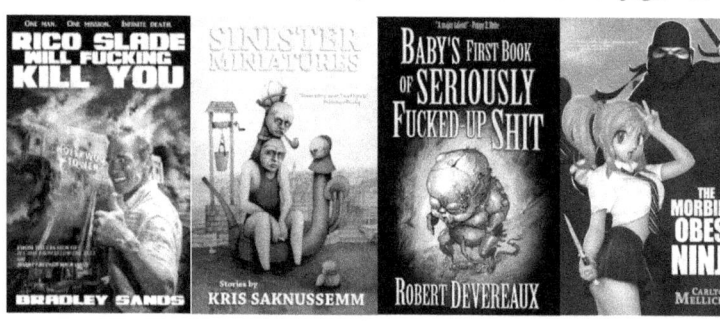

BB-119 **"Rico Slade Will Fucking Kill You" Bradley Sands** — Rico Slade is an action hero. Rico Slade can rip out a throat with his bare hands. Rico Slade's favorite food is the honey-roasted peanut. Rico Slade will fucking kill everyone. A novel. **122 pages $8**

BB-120 **"Sinister Miniatures" Kris Saknussemm** — The definitive collection of short fiction by Kris Saknussemm, confirming that he is one of the best, most daring writers of the weird to emerge in the twenty-first century. **180 pages $11**

BB-121 **"Baby's First Book of Seriously Fucked up Shit" Robert Devereaux** — Ten stories of the strange, the gross, and the just plain fucked up from one of the most original voices in horror. **176 pages $11**

BB-122 **"The Morbidly Obese Ninja" Carlton Mellick III** — These days, if you want to run a successful company . . . you're going to need a lot of ninjas. **92 pages $8**

BB-123 **"Abortion Arcade" Cameron Pierce** — An intoxicating blend of body horror and midnight movie madness, reminiscent of early David Lynch and the splatterpunks at their most sublime. **172 pages $11**

BB-124 **"Black Hole Blues" Patrick Wensink** — A hilarious double helix of country music and physics. **196 pages $11**

BB-125 **"Barbarian Beast Bitches of the Badlands" Carlton Mellick III** — Three prequels and sequels to *Warrior Wolf Women of the Wasteland*. **284 pages $13**

BB-126 **"The Traveling Dildo Salesman" Kevin L. Donihe** — A nightmare comedy about destiny, faith, and sex toys. Also featuring Donihe's most lurid and infamous short stories: *Milky Agitation, Two-Way Santa, The Helen Mower, Living Room Zombies,* and *Revenge of the Living Masturbation Rag.* **108 pages $8**

BB-127 **"Metamorphosis Blues" Bruce Taylor** — Enter a land of love beasts, intergalactic cowboys, and rock 'n roll. A land where Sears Catalogs are doorways to insanity and men keep mysterious black boxes. Welcome to the monstrous mind of Mr. Magic Realism. **136 pages $11**

BB-128 **"The Driver's Guide to Hitting Pedestrians" Andersen Prunty** — A pocket guide to the twenty-three most painful things in life, written by the most well-adjusted man in the universe. **108 pages $8**

BB-129 **"Island of the Super People" Kevin Shamel** — Four students and their anthropology professor journey to a remote island to study its indigenous population. But this is no ordinary native culture. They're super heroes and villains with flesh costumes and out-landish abilities like self-detonation, musical eyelashes, and microwave hands. **194 pages $11**

BB-130 **"Fantastic Orgy" Carlton Mellick III** — Shark Sex, mutant cats, and strange sexually transmitted diseases. Featuring the stories: *Candy-coated, Ear Cat, Fantastic Orgy, City Hobgoblins,* and *Porno in August.* **136 pages $9**

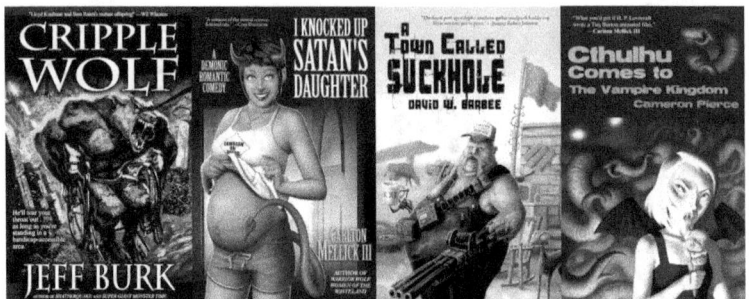

BB-131 **"Cripple Wolf" Jeff Burk** — Part man. Part wolf. 100% crippled. Also including *Punk Rock Nursing Home, Adrift with Space Badgers, Cook for Your Life, Just Another Day in the Park, Frosty and the Full Monty*, and *House of Cats*. **152 pages $10**

BB-132 **"I Knocked Up Satan's Daughter" Carlton Mellick III** — An adorable, violent, fantastical love story. A romantic comedy for the bizarro fiction reader. **152 pages $10**

BB-133 **"A Town Called Suckhole" David W. Barbee** — Far into the future, in the nuclear bowels of post-apocalyptic Dixie, there is a town. A town of derelict mobile homes, ancient junk, and mutant wildlife. A town of slack jawed rednecks who bask in the splendors of moonshine and mud boggin'. A town dedicated to the bloody and demented legacy of the Old South. A town called Suckhole. **144 pages $10**

BB-134 **"Cthulhu Comes to the Vampire Kingdom" Cameron Pierce** — What you'd get if H. P. Lovecraft wrote a Tim Burton animated film. **148 pages $11**

BB-135 **"I am Genghis Cum" Violet LeVoit** — From the savage Arctic tundra to post-partum mutations to your missing daughter's unmarked grave, join visionary madwoman Violet LeVoit in this non-stop eight-story onslaught of full-tilt Bizarro punk lit thrills. **124 pages $9**

BB-136 **"Haunt" Laura Lee Bahr** — A tripping-balls Los Angeles noir, where a mysterious dame drags you through a time-warping Bizarro hall of mirrors. **316 pages $13**

BB-137 **"Amazing Stories of the Flying Spaghetti Monster" edited by Cameron Pierce** — Like an all-spaghetti evening of Adult Swim, the Flying Spaghetti Monster will show you the many realms of His Noodly Appendage. Learn of those who worship him and the lives he touches in distant, mysterious ways. **228 pages $12**

BB-138 **"Wave of Mutilation" Douglas Lain** — A dream-pop exploration of modern architecture and the American identity, *Wave of Mutilation* is a Zen finger trap for the 21st century. **100 pages $8**

BB-139 **"Hooray for Death!" Mykle Hansen** — Famous Author Mykle Hansen draws unconventional humor from deaths tiny and large, and invites you to laugh while you can. **128 pages $10**

BB-140 **"Hypno-hog's Moonshine Monster Jamboree" Andrew Goldfarb** — Hicks, Hogs, Horror! Goldfarb is back with another strange illustrated tale of backwoods weirdness. **120 pages $9**

BB-141 **"Broken Piano For President" Patrick Wensink** — A comic masterpiece about the fast food industry, booze, and the necessity to choose happiness over work and security. **372 pages $15**

BB-142 **"Please Do Not Shoot Me in the Face" Bradley Sands** — A novel in three parts, *Please Do Not Shoot Me in the Face: A Novel*, is the story of one boy detective, the worst ninja in the world, and the great American fast food wars. It is a novel of loss, destruction, and--incredibly--genuine hope. **224 pages $12**

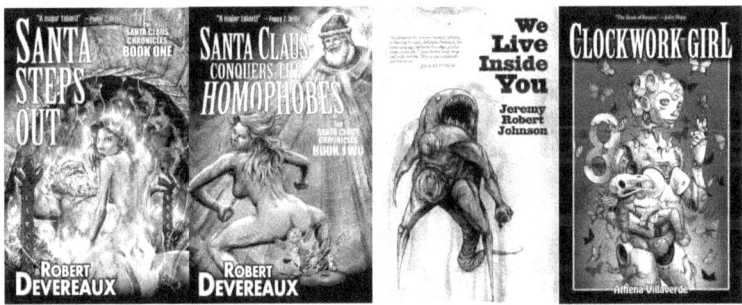

BB-143 **"Santa Steps Out" Robert Devereaux** — Sex, Death, and Santa Claus ... The ultimate erotic Christmas story is back. **294 pages $13**

BB-144 **"Santa Conquers the Homophobes" Robert Devereaux** — "I wish I could hope to ever attain one-thousandth the perversity of Robert Devereaux's toenail clippings." - Poppy Z. Brite **316 pages $13**

BB-145 **"We Live Inside You" Jeremy Robert Johnson** — "Jeremy Robert Johnson is dancing to a way different drummer. He loves language, he loves the edge, and he loves us people. These stories have range and style and wit. This is entertainment... and literature."- Jack Ketchum **188 pages $11**

BB-146 **"Clockwork Girl" Athena Villaverde** — Urban fairy tales for the weird girl in all of us. Like a combination of Francesca Lia Block, Charles de Lint, Kathe Koja, Tim Burton, and Hayao Miyazaki, her stories are cute, kinky, edgy, magical, provocative, and strange, full of poetic imagery and vicious sexuality. **160 pages $10**

BB-147 **"Armadillo Fists" Carlton Mellick III** — A weird-as-hell gangster story set in a world where people drive giant mechanical dinosaurs instead of cars. **168 pages $11**

BB-148 **"Gargoyle Girls of Spider Island" Cameron Pierce** — Four college seniors venture out into open waters for the tropical party weekend of a lifetime. Instead of a teenage sex fantasy, they find themselves in a nightmare of pirates, sharks, and sex-crazed monsters. **100 pages $8**

BB-149 **"The Handsome Squirm" by Carlton Mellick III** — Like Franz Kafka's *The Trial* meets an erotic body horror version of *The Blob*. **158 pages $11**

BB-150 **"Tentacle Death Trip" Jordan Krall** — It's *Death Race 2000* meets H. P. Lovecraft in bizarro author Jordan Krall's best and most suspenseful work to date. **224 pages $12**

BB-151 **"The Obese" Nick Antosca** — Like Alfred Hitchcock's *The Birds*... but with obese people. **108 pages $10**

BB-152 **"All-Monster Action!" Cody Goodfellow** — The world gave him a blank check and a demand: Create giant monsters to fight our wars. But Dr. Otaku was not satisfied with mere chaos and mass destruction.... **216 pages $12**

BB-153 **"Ugly Heaven" Carlton Mellick III** — Heaven is no longer a paradise. It was once a blissful utopia full of wonders far beyond human comprehension. But the afterlife is now in ruins. It has become an ugly, lonely wasteland populated by strange monstrous beasts, masturbating angels, and sad man-like beings wallowing in the remains of the once-great Kingdom of God. **106 pages $8**

BB-154 **"Space Walrus" Kevin L. Donihe** — Walter is supposed to go where no walrus has ever gone before, but all this astronaut walrus really wants is to take it easy on the intense training, escape the chimpanzee bullies, and win the love of his human trainer Dr. Stephanie. **160 pages $11**

BB-155 **"Unicorn Battle Squad" Kirsten Alene** — Mutant unicorns. A palace with a thousand human legs. The most powerful army on the planet. **192 pages $11**

BB-156 **"Kill Ball" Carlton Mellick III** — In a city where all humans live inside of plastic bubbles, exotic dancers are being murdered in the rubbery streets by a mysterious stalker known only as Kill Ball. **134 pages $10**

BB-157 **"Die You Doughnut Bastards" Cameron Pierce** — The bacon storm is rolling in. We hear the grease and sugar beat against the roof and windows. The doughnut people are attacking. We press close together, forgetting for a moment that we hate each other. **196 pages $11**

BB-158 **"Tumor Fruit" Carlton Mellick III** — Eight desperate castaways find themselves stranded on a mysterious deserted island. They are surrounded by poisonous blue plants and an ocean made of acid. Ravenous creatures lurk in the toxic jungle. The ghostly sound of crying babies can be heard on the wind. **310 pages $13**

BB-159 **"Thunderpussy" David W. Barbee** — When it comes to high-tech global espionage, only one man has the balls to save humanity from the world's most powerful bastards. He's Declan Magpie Bruce, Agent 00X. **136 pages $11**

BB-160 **"Papier Mâché Jesus" Kevin L. Donihe** — Donihe's surreal wit and beautiful mind-bending imagination is on full display with stories such as All Children Go to Hell, Happiness is a Warm Gun, and Swimming in Endless Night. **154 pages $11**

BB-161 **"Cuddly Holocaust" Carlton Mellick III** — The war between humans and toys has come to an end. The toys won. **172 pages $11**

BB-162 **"Hammer Wives" Carlton Mellick III** — Fish-eyed mutants, oceans of insects, and flesh-eating women with hammers for heads. Hammer Wives collects six of his most popular novelettes and short stories. **152 pages $10**